Ursa Steel

A Sci-Fi Anthology

Jacob Russell Dring

Foreword

Every story in this collection occurs in the same fictional universe/distant future in which humanity's existence is reliant on its military industry and space exploration.

Within *Ursa Steel* there is camaraderie and honor, but there is also horror and despair. Each story stands alone with different themes, levels of intensity, and characters. The variety contained is sure to appease anyone seeking an adventure.

Contents

Harvest Death

"Growth for the sake of growth is the ideology of the cancer cell."

Edward Abbey

1

Natives of J-726 sharpened tools and chittered through lipless, toothy mouths as the sound of thunder came overhead. It was a sunny day, the seventh hour of the dwarf planet's nineteen-hour rotation. No storm clouds, no darkening of the periwinkle sky. The sound was raucous and staccato. Natives emerged from dense hedgerows to peer up, past the shade provided by jungle canopies.

Through a layer of cirrus clouds descended a structure with two fixed wings and—

"Remember your training, and the three do's," Dillon Badge's XO shouted inside the VTOL, his raspy voice straining to be heard over the pulsing thunder of its dual thrusters. "Shoot anything with four arms, announce your reloads, and evacuate the wounded."

"And the don'ts?" Badge's CO shouted, standing beside the XO, also gripping an overhead rung. Unlike

Badge and his fellow twenty-nine infantrymen, harnessed to seats lining the inner bulkheads of the VTOL.

Grizzled rifleman vet and ex-Mech pilot Gunnery Sergeant Patton Beck nodded at his CO. They exchanged fleeting smirks before Beck shouted one more line piggybacked by his CO's own voice. Lieutenant Sean Greenwood was six years Beck's junior, his voice a touch smoother, but no less commanding.

"*Don't* kill, then *don't* live!"

In unison, the thirty infantrymen shouted the next line of the mantra with their superiors.

"The Fleet has no time for cold feet!"

Beneath the aircraft, the atmosphere of J-726 awaited them, and was anything but cold. Deemed *Jade* by non-officers, the white-mottled green speck among the stars was aptly nicknamed. Humid and temperate, a tropical climate likened to the Cambodian jungles back home, or the Lumira swamps on Canis Nine.

At least it was breathable.

A purer air supply than even Brosia. Badge had never been, but whenever anxiety hit him like a freighter, he would disassociate and project himself onto that planet. Fourth from the sun in the Trion system. He couldn't afford it, but that didn't keep his mind from working the way it did.

Unfortunately, now was not one of those times.

There wasn't a second to spare, not for daydreaming or escapism.

As if to confirm this, the inside of the VTOL turned green. Thirty seconds to touch-down. Half his platoon aboard the craft had only been on simulated drops, which made this their first ITF one. Badge was in that boat, but he had confidence in his superiors.

Even if they, supposedly as well, didn't know *why* exactly the Fleet was sending them to Jade. Without explosives, and the directive *not* to damage any trees. He wondered how feasible that was, considering eighty percent of the planet's surface was wooded. Whatever prized resource lay in Jade's trees, it was apparently more valuable than two companies' lives.

The VTOL's fixed wings bucked as its pilot leveled it out, managing a gust of wind that rattled its frame. Badge's teeth would have chattered to the point of breaking had it not been for his rubber mouthpiece. The other twenty-nine infantrymen harnessed to their seats, lining the VTOL's bulkheads, were equally grateful. Even if it meant praying out loud a little difficult.

Simulations, real as they might seem, could never replicate the inescapable dread that came with an ITF drop. But that was true with anything; nothing compared to a live, in the flesh experience.

Combat deployment especially.

When the green turned red, Badge's heart skipped a beat and his empty hands yearned to hold his weapon. Instead he clutched the three-point harness binding him to his seat, and closed his eyes.

The gentle, pure air on Brosia swept across his face, cooling sweat. Transparent waters awaited him, and an ecology devoid of predators or insects. A soft voice called his name, and he turned to set his eyes upon the woman of his dreams, Ana Koczian. Three days ago, before Gamma Company deployed from orbit, she had videoed him proof of her Mech pilot license. But here, on Brosia, she was free from the bulky gear that a Mech pilot had to wear in the cockpit. Her swimsuit was a startling blue, matching the hue of her eyes.

When she called his name again, it was deep and gruff. His eyes opened and Badge's XO stood above him, shouting "Private" until reality came back to him.

"Get your shit together and gear up!"

"Yes, Sergeant!" Badge replied, realizing that his harness had been retracted, and the deep red hue of the VTOL's interior was gone. Replaced by the raw daylight flooding in through the lowered ramp to his far left. He hoisted himself off the seat, turned, and retrieved his weapon from the rack above it.

"Move your ass, Private!" Beck barked.

"Moving, sir!"

The second Badge's hands had found solace in the grooves of his Imperator assault rifle, he had forgotten about Brosia, and damn near banished the existence of his ex-fiancé from his mind.

All was right in the world, he told himself.

Badge had never been a good liar.

Outside the VTOL, twenty soldiers had already amassed, moving like a wave of a green-camouflaged, helmeted ants through a field of elbow-high tallgrass.

Some ten stragglers eventually made their way out of the craft, their minds lulling just as Badge's had.

So much for no time to daydream.

His shame as an infantryman for the mighty Fleet dissipated once he was among his fellow troops. Wading through tallgrass from another planet, one only scouted by Fleet science officers with a lightly armed escort. No wonder they were slaughtered, and only their transmitted findings survived.

Jade natives swarmed the far treeline, across a field of mixed foliage seventy meters wide. This shrubland seemed to extend for nearly half a kilometer east of them, the same direction that four other platoons in individual VTOLs prepared for touch-down. They were each a klick apart, with a dyad of Mechs between first and second, and third and fourth.

Badge hoped that four Mechs per company would suffice against the enemy, given the Fleet's prohibition of explosives. To his knowledge, this meant that technicians aboard the Mech drop-pods had removed every missile from the machines prepping deployment. HE and incendiary rounds for their Autocannons had also been shelved, in favor of shot and slugs.

At least the Mech equivalent of buckshot was enough to shred half a platoon in one trigger-pull, so Badge's hope was not completely null and void.

"Onward!" Lt. Greenwood shouted, as a third of his platoon had lulled in the tallgrass. They flinched and resumed movement, marching toward the front of the field, where the seventy-meter shrubland awaited them, and their enemy teemed among towering trees, beneath dense jungle canopies, on the other side.

Both Beck and Greenwood's positions were highlighted as green carets along the top of every soldier's visor HUD. The heads-up display also offered a moving compass and a blue dot for the position of friendly vehicles, including aircraft and Mechs, within a hundred-meter radius.

Badge noticed that Lt. Greenwood was still far behind the bulk of his platoon. The last man off the VTOL, as per protocol. He glanced over his shoulder as he approached the edge of the tallgrass, pausing about ten meters from it. Nine other infantrymen were playing catch-up, not including the Lieutenant. He had begun to wade through the field, behind him the flattened LZ. Tallgrass already matted to the earth and singed from the fusion heat of the VTOL's thrusters briefly caught fire before the sheer force of propulsion put it out.

The elevation indicator attached to the blue dot on Badge's HUD was as relieving as the sight itself. The VTOL was ascending, its pilot mindful of a nearby copse. Detached from the fuller, vaster jungle across the field, the small gathering of trees had not been assessed as a threat.

From its layered canopies suddenly emerged a throng of natives, their lean, green-skinned bodies hurtling through the clear air, before landing on the VTOL's left wing. Badge's relief was short-lived. His breath cut shy in his throat, whereas a handful of other infantrymen shouted and some pointed.

Beck was at the head of their platoon, awaiting his CO clear of the tallgrass. Now he turned, and Greenwood also pitched his attention skyward.

Three of the eight four-armed, vaguely humanoid creatures didn't land properly, falling to the tallgrass below. The other five clambered on top of the VTOL, its wings suddenly bucking. The pilot was either aware of the attack and attempting to shed the natives from his craft, or he was struggling to rebalance it.

Greenwood wanted to command his snipers to target the creatures, but he bit his tongue and silently cursed his superiors. They had insisted only riflemen, grenadiers, and medics to be deployed for the first wave on Jade. Two medics per platoon, and five grenadiers—the latter weren't even permitted to carry explosives, so they were designated heavy-weapons.

No snipers, as his superiors had *determined* that combat would strictly be mid- to close-range, and the sheer numbers of the enemy would render sharpshooters an overwhelmed unit.

"To hell with this," Greenwood growled through his teeth. He turned and beckoned at his platoon, who watched their VTOL in awe.

One of the four-armed natives had attempted to destroy a thruster on the left wing, striking at it with two wielded machete-like tools. But it lost its footing and its other arms slapped at the bulbous thruster, for traction. Then a fusion pulse incinerated it, and cauterized limbs fell to the terrain below.

A few soldiers cheered.

"Grenadiers!" Greenwood shouted.

Five men rushed toward their CO, each wielding a Thunder LMG. To call the weapon a *light* machinegun seemed criminal, given their tremendous weight and firepower. Grenadiers were thus the most robust men in a platoon, as no average soldier could singlehandedly operate such a weapons system.

"Tight bursts!" Greenwood ordered, pointing up at the VTOL.

It was gaining altitude, but not in a leveled manner. Its wings continued to buck every few seconds, and the craft as a whole was slowly spinning.

Three of the five grenadiers began firing in two-round bursts, eyeing their targets through projected red-dot optics. At a range of nearly sixty meters and increasing, these shots weren't hard to make, but the elevation, angle, and small targets aboard a friendly craft exacerbated their aim.

The other two grenadiers fanned out, but not to target the natives attacking the VTOL.

"Ten o'clock!" one of them shouted.

"One, no, two o'clock!" The other sounded off.

Greenwood realized that the three natives which had not landed on the VTOL were now charging them through the tallgrass. Meanwhile, the grenadiers firing at the four maintaining balance atop the aircraft stayed focused.

"LT," Beck said, touching the side of his helmet to trigger the com-link between him and Greenwood. "They've broken cover!"

Thirty meters behind Beck, Greenwood couldn't see the treeline, but didn't doubt his comrade.

"Four riflemen, on me!" Greenwood shouted, gesturing in the air. He didn't need to privately reply to Beck, which he knew the XO would appreciate. Then he thrusted his hand away from him, and bellowed: "First Platoon, *onward*!"

Beck hollered a wordless war-cry as he led the bulk of his men out of the tallgrass, and into the shrubland between them and the far treeline. The enemy had begun to emerge from their jungle cover, making no sounds themselves, and moving like a swarm of carnivorous insects.

Though torn between staying with his XO or joining Lt. Greenwood's request for four riflemen, Badge's indecision evaporated against his will. A passing soldier bumped shoulders with him, a young face he knew even in a blur of adrenaline and anxiety. Private Sebastian Holloway, arguably the greenest infantryman in all of Gamma Company. His only rival for that shameful title was Private Ira Harrison, Ithaca Company, the second wave set to assail Jade's southern hemisphere in three hours' time.

Holloway must have wanted to retreat from facing the enemy horde that charged across the shrubland, instead choosing the lesser evil by joining their CO in the tallgrass. Badge didn't blame him, and while he wasn't as familiar with his comrade as he wished he was, there was no ill will.

Badge hoped Holloway saw it home, and not in a light-reflective black bag.

"Badge, goddammit, *forward*!"

He recognized the voice, as Corporal Trevor McLeod. One of the best damn riflemen he had ever befriended, though the experienced soldier would likely consider them as no more than acquaintances. Brothers-in-arms at best, a title Badge would proudly wear.

McLeod was one of the only reasons Badge had survived boot, and had honed his marksmanship skills in the year that followed. Since, the man, who was now eight years his senior at thirty-six, had ascended from Private to PFC to Corporal, and become Badge's sort of guardian angel.

A fistful of Badge's uniform later, and McLeod was essentially dragging the Private through the tall-grass. They breached the edge, McLeod let go, and waved over his head, shouting "forward" in a gritty, thundering Scottish voice.

Behind Badge, two more infantrymen—both medics—tentatively advanced. If anyone had the right to harbor fear, it was them. Less experienced in weapons handling than anyone else in the company, medics were ironically the bravest of the bunch.

Theoretically.

Somehow, not being fired upon by enemy weapons but instead charged at by silent, humanoid, four-armed carnivores of an unexplored planet was far more terrifying.

A breeze swept overhead, tingling the hairs on Badge's scalp, and he recalled his vision of Brosia. He recalled the peace that he imagined existed on its surface, and the sheer concept of him reuniting with Ms. Koczian was enough to spur him into action.

Dillon Badge was not a coward.

He was only human.

In that instant, he remembered what he was fighting for—a better future for the human race. Whatever resources on J-726 that Fleet Intelligence wanted so damn bad *had* to be worth the lives of 150 men—twice that, if Ithaca Company was considered. And more, quite possibly, in future waves.

Badge held onto this about as tightly as he did his Imperator, the Fleet's standard-issue bullpup assault rifle. Once twenty paces into the shrubland, he hunkered behind a fallen tree, its decaying trunk the width of two robust grenadiers strapped together. Sufficient cover for a moment, to gather one's wits and assess the enemy. Badge shouldered his compact weapon and put his eye behind the mounted 3x optic.

His helmet's upper-face visor linked with the optic and marked targets as they rushed through foliage that could be likened to prehistoric Earth. Little red circles appeared around their ovoid heads, keeping them marked even if they vanished from his line-of-sight. Anyone else in the platoon that tracked a target via his weapons optic, those that were equipped with them—

SMGs and shotguns weren't—synchronized across every visor.

The amount of red rings on his HUD were almost dizzying. They multiplied like wildfire. Or a viral growth.

"Weapons *free!*" Beck roared, to Badge's far right, standing clear of the tree log's myriad, decaying roots. His enunciation of "free" was so deep that the vowels caught in his throat and came out like a buzzsaw.

Badge had never been more motivated.

He sprang from cover for a better stance and opened fire. McLeod followed suit, briefly stunned by his comrade's sudden burst of conviction.

Half the platoon opened up on the charging enemy. Natives sprang from fern-like flora the size of small cars, shuddering leaves in their wake. Each creature stood seven feet head to toe, with an upper armspan of an equally tall professional basketball player. Their second set of arms, protruding from the pits, were about six inches shorter than the uppers. They were used for maneuvering and striking or seizing their opponents, whereas their uppers wielded machete-like weapons, or clubs similar to spiked maces except composed from some sort of bone.

As Badge witnessed one of his comrades rush to meet the enemy, adrenaline conquering intelligence, he realized something. The clubs wielded by the natives weren't made of bone, or rock, but he reckoned wood.

The same lumber that composed the planet's trees. Perhaps not all of them, as the clubs seemed too rigid and unyielding to submit to decay.

Unlike the log he stood behind.

Badge wanted to fire at the creature that his comrade collided with, but they were too close together. The rifleman wielded a Cutter SMG, the same weapon that dangled from Beck's kit belt. It was some of their primary weapons, despite its compacter size. The automatic PDW had a faster rate-of-fire than the Imperator, and was affixed with a seven-inch serrated bayonet.

The soldier used it in that instant to gut his enemy, sawing through the native's leathery green skin with what seemed like ease. Adrenaline made everything *seem* easy, though. Steam and a rank, yellowish fluid spilled out of the native's stomach.

It all happened so damn fast.

The creature overhanded its club, both hands from its upper arms wielding the weapon. The bulbous, jagged end of the weapon struck the soldier's helmet, cleaving it like a split melon. If it really was made of the same lumber that composed Jade's trees, the club's durability made a wandering part of Badge's mind think that *this* was the Fleet's sought-after resource.

In the next blink of an eye, the entirety of Badge's focus was on the verdant battlefield before him.

The club had lodged into the poor soldier's skull after cleaving his helmet, and when the eviscerated native yanked its arms to the side, Badge watched his comrade's head open up like a split pumpkin. Mush spewed out, splashing a nearby leaf the size of a dog. The man's body crumpled and the native, despite missing its innards, shrieked through a gaping mouth lined with short but sharp, haphazardly arranged, crocodilian teeth.

Badge's stomach turned.

"Keep – firing!" McLeod shouted inches from him, his inner-ear protection filtering sounds of a lower frequency than gunfire.

Badge gulped, nodded more to himself than anyone else, and regained his focus. He fired a burst from the Imperator at the native he'd just watched slay one of his brothers-in-arms, and caught it in the shoulder with a cluster of 6.8mm rounds. The creature flinched, spun, and charged him from twenty meters away, descending to all fours—sixes?—through a quilt of foliage. It must have abandoned its weapon in order to move so nimbly, and fear crept back into Badge's system like a plague.

He began to backpedal, tracking the red-haloed enemy through his visor, weapon slightly lowered for better visibility.

The platoon was engaging the enemy with better efficiency than Badge might have expected, after witnessing such a horror. The wave of natives was thinning, and nearly a dozen riflemen were slowly pushing forward. The covering fire of two grenadiers on overwatch from the edge of the tallgrass slightly above and behind the rest of the men certainly helped.

Every .308 Magnum round from the LMGs either put fist-sized holes into the enemy, or chewed through their foliage cover.

Beck dropped to a knee behind the mess of up-ended roots from the log to reload his weapon. A drum-fed assault shotgun, the notorious 12-gauge Reaper. Everyone in Gamma company knew that the Gunnery Sergeant loaded his sixteen-round drum with alternating buckshot and slugs, in two-round intervals. Then he engaged the enemy tactically, according to their range and what was chambered; if slugs were up but the enemy was within twenty meters, he'd switch to his Cutter and put the SMG to use. If buckshot was chambered but his target was beyond twenty meters, he'd burst-fire the Cutter until the job was done.

Realizing—as he loaded individual shells into the drum of the Reaper, his right knee sinking into the firm grassy soil—that the presence of grenadiers meant one thing. They must have shed the VTOL of its attackers, or neutralized the ground threats. Either-or; Beck prayed both, noticing that the elevation and range on the VTOL's blue-dot HUD indicator was dramatically increasing. Unfortunately, Lt. Greenwood's caret had not gotten any closer to his position.

He finished reloading, minded the hosing gunfire from the nearest grenadier's LMG, and pushed forward.

Badge noticed his XO's advancement, but a split-second later, his target erupted from the groin-high foliage on the other side of the log, swiping at him and displaying its teeth. A hissing sound exited its horrid mouth, paired with a stench not unlike rotting meat. Badge recoiled, firing his weapon in full-auto as he fell. Bullets climbed up the creature's midsection, which was already dripping viscera from its last victim's bayonet charge.

As it came down on top of him, knocking his weapon out of his hands, McLeod stepped forward to kick it in what would be its left ribcage. The force from the strike and the sole of his infantry boot knocked the native off of Badge. A flurry of green limbs rustled the surrounding flora as it regained its footing.

McLeod went to fire but only two rounds exited his Imperator before the magazine went dry. Smoke spewed from its locked-open breech, and birdcage muzzle, but he didn't hesitate to let it sag on its sling as he drew his sidearm and locked his elbow. The native hissed and would have lunged at him, over Badge's supine body, but—

McLeod squeezed the trigger to his pistol with such speed and firmness that the native never had a chance. Ten-mil hollowpoints ruptured its skull and put blossoming holes in its narrow neck, dropping the creature in two seconds.

The sallow blood that poured from its wounds and misted the air had its own reek to it, which made human gore seem aromatic by comparison.

McLeod holstered his pistol and helped Badge to his feet.

"These fuckers are resilient, aren't they?" he said, stanch-faced but not devoid of distress.

"Resilient, but mortal." The Gunnery Sergeant's voice was unmistakable even amid spurts of gunfire. Beck appeared behind McLeod, and nodded at the slain creature to Badge's left. His voice was almost mellow, with the vaguest hint of dry humor. "Good work. Now stow that pea-shooter and move on."

McLeod offered the rattled Dillon Badge a tiny smirk, nudged him in the arm, and then gestured with a nod of his head. Badge hunted for his Imperator, scooped it up, and followed McLeod over the log.

A quick survey of the vegetated gorge between the tallgrass field and the jungle yielded relieving results. More than half of the marked targets had vanished, which counted as casualties on the enemy's side. The remaining ones, unfortunately, knew no concept of surrender or retreat. They pressed, despite being outnumbered and outgunned.

Badge witnessed a white-sleeved medic step in to assist the slaughter of an enemy native. The four-armed creature had been swinging not one but *two* machetes in both hands, while its lower pair were injured; one arm hung limply, likely fractured somehow, and the other had been blown-off at the elbow. The medic and rifleman hosed down the creature with bullets, each soldier wielding a Murmur SBR. The short-barreled rifles were integrally suppressed and standard for medics who didn't want a bayoneted SMG. Their rate-of-fire was insane, and ideal for close quarters.

The two infantrymen clearly had no qualm with ganging up on the hopeless native, despite its imposing appearance and fearlessness.

When Badge's foot landed in what he suspected was a soft part of the earth, like a puddle of mud or dung, he grimaced and looked down. His expression soured when he realized it was the chest cavity of a fellow soldier. The man's head was missing, likely cleaved off by an enemy machete. The wound in his chest included a staved sternum and crushed organs.

Had they already been crushed by a native's club, or not until now by Badge's boot, he couldn't be sure. His stomach knotted and he forced down vomit as he staggered out of the mess.

"Oh, fuck me," a soldier's voice muttered, catching a brief silence between staccato gunfire in the area.

Badge turned and saw Private Edwin Araújo drop his Imperator to kneel by a severed head six feet away. When Araújo's despair-stricken face lifted to make eye contact with the nearest person, in this case Badge, a tear plopped onto a blood-misted leaf.

"It's Rianne," Araújo said. He realized that Badge didn't recognize the name. Araújo almost sneered at him. "*PFC* Orville Rianne."

"I-I'm sorry." Badge said, trying not to shrug. He glanced around, made brief eye contact with McLeod, who was at this point navigating the brush to confirm kills with occasional double-taps from his weapon.

Then Badge joined Araújo, and reluctantly placed his hands on the severed soldier's head, to turn the dead, fear-frozen face toward the ground. Badge tried to comfort Araújo with as much genuine concern as he could muster. He had to detach himself slightly so as to not be mired by despair, even if he didn't personally know PFC Rianne.

"Leave him, Edwin. We've taken the field, Fleet medevac will handle the dead—properly."

"I *grew up with him*, Badge." Araújo's voice trembled. Tears streaked his cheeks in many rivulets. "I knew him since he was *six*. I...I'm friends with his cousin, I w-was at his wedding, I..."

Badge breathed arduously through his nostrils. He mustered the strength to be an asshole in the situation.

"Keyword, Private. *Knew*." Badge grabbed Araújo's uniform by the collar. "Now, if you want to keep *knowing* your fellow infantrymen, get on your feet. And *move*. Otherwise, climb in a bodybag with Rianne and fail to tell his family that he died *bravely*."

During Badge's literally painstaking speech, Araújo experienced a range of emotions in rapid form. First, anger and resentment. Then, more forwardly, grief. Followed by an inward shame of understanding. And lastly, a sense of acceptance.

He processed it as a good soldier, a logical human, should.

Sniffling, Araújo nodded, slid his hands off of Rianne's severed head, whose face was now facing the ground, and stood. Araújo wobbled briefly before returning the Imperator to his hands, and regarding Badge with a bittersweet nod. He walked past him, advancing toward the treeline with his fellow infantrymen.

Badge let out a deep, wavering breath.

He stood, himself teetering ever so briefly. He cursed under his breath, lifted his head, and adjusted his helmet. A passing grenadier wielding an LMG with good barrel discipline gave him a respectful nod. Then he crossed himself after glancing at the decapitated soldier.

Badge steadied his breathing and surveyed the shrubland between tallgrass and treeline. The sound of sporadic gunfire was all but dead now. They had, in fact, taken the field and cleared their LZ. He noticed Greenwood's caret on his HUD coming in from the rear, a good sign.

The second he noticed the Lieutenant clear the edge of the tallgrass, accompanied by a grenadier and rifleman, Badge turned—minding his feet of Rianne's remains.

In that instant he bumped into McLeod, who apparently had heard his exchange with Araújo.

There was pride on his weathered, scar-cheeked face. Badge had not seem him so impressed with someone else in a long time, but this moment was different than boot. A sullenness to his eyes lurked and gave him an air of vulnerability that Badge seldom saw in the man.

"Step up like that, when bullets are flying, and you'll clear a rank."

Badge nodded grimly.

"Remember. Higher rank ain't about bossing other guys around. If you're really of merit, it's about inspiring courage."

"Yes, sir."

McLeod wasn't blind to the inner war Badge was fighting, but respected it with all his heart.

He looked around, and nodded a few times.

"Carry on."

"Thank you, Corporal," Badge muttered.

He attempted to muster a modicum of positive emotion. It barely carried through.

McLeod appreciated it nonetheless, and followed the Private toward the treeline. Along the hedgerow bordering the towering, narrow-trunked trees like a waist-high fence of overlapping foliage, the platoon had gathered. Most of them, anyway.

Beck was performing a silent head-count when Greenwood arrived, adding a grenadier and rifleman to their numbers.

"How's it looking, boss?" Greenwood asked the XO, pleased to see no sign of injury on him.

Beck finished counting before answering *his* boss, equally relieved to see the Lieutenant untouched by wounds. A scarce splatter of the enemy's distinctive blood did, however, add some color to his otherwise drab uniform.

"Relatively good, which is hard to admit," Beck said, his voice lower than usual. He exchanged shoulder-pats with Greenwood as they ventured away from the platoon, enough to be out of earshot.

"Cut the shit, Beck, how are we doing?" Greenwood asked.

The Gunnery Sergeant shook his head.

"If we go by the numbers, it was a victory, through and through."

Greenwood's brow furrowed. He wasn't used to Beck being this even-tempered, much less well-spoken. He was a brute of a man more often than not, which wasn't to say that Greenwood ever believed him to be undereducated. Clearly, something grave troubled him. Something Greenwood had not grasped on his way over.

"But, sir," Beck said. "The men are rattled. Our losses...I count six dead. *Six*, against the *horde* that charged us."

"As you said...the numbers..." Greenwood began to say "good" but the word didn't fit right on his tongue.

"Right. But the enemy, they charged us—in the open. Clubs and, like, machetes. That's it. No projectiles, no armor."

"For once, the intel was right," Greenwood tried to smirk. Sweat still dripped from his face, and the humidity of the climate clung to his skin. What made this worse was the stench; of the fallen enemy, and their own casualties. Death occupied the air in a way that violated everyone's senses with ease. No matter how far they were from the bodies.

"What the *intel* didn't quite piece together, LT," Beck said, through his teeth, the anger itching for a release. "Is how *tough* these sumbitches are."

Greenwood nodded, and looked around. Behind him, particularly. He realized, quickly that he had not surveyed the expanse of foliage more than merely avoiding large obstacles on his way over here. He began to speak, to reply to the XO, but his voice fell short.

Something caught his eye.

He wandered over to a tangle of limbs that belonged to two corpses which flattered a large bush.

When Greenwood hunkered over, he recoiled from the power of the smell. The sight alone would stick in his brain for a long time, he feared.

A rifleman and a native had clashed. The soldier's chest was cleaved, from shoulder to sternum, his ribs broken like sticks, his organs bisected and having spilled out through the gaping V-shaped wound. At its base, the enemy's machete-like weapon was still stuck in the flesh. The iron-colored blade was nearly four feet long, and the grip about eight inches, composed of some sort of wood.

Greenwood tried to avoid making eye contact with the dead infantryman; he knew that Beck, being Beck, had already identified their casualties. Ashamedly, Greenwood now avoided this, to save his own conscience, though he knew it wouldn't last.

The soldier's gaze was upturned to the bloodshot whites of his eyes, only a glimpse of his irises visible.

2

There was something dampening, or even demoralizing, about calling a pair of war machines, or their pilots for that matter, a *duo*. Or a *duet*, especially. So *dyad* found its way into the mix, and everybody was happy. Even the women agreed. And a quarter of all Mech pilots, according to Ursa Steel statistics, were female.

Women had come a long way for equality, but still there was a lot of pressure on female machineheads. Ana Koczian had proven herself to the moons and back, though. Crew that knew her, or had at least heard of her, owed their respect. And their faith.

She couldn't help but wonder if any of this had ever reached her ex-fiancé. Ursa Steel and Fleet infantry mixed like apples and oranges. Strategies were different, communications were different. She just hoped that, wherever he was, Dillon Badge didn't resent her for ending their relationship due to the strains of combat and distance. She imagined that seas of stars now separated them, but after landing on J-726 in her Middleweight, she was glad. The farther the better.

This place was beautiful from orbit, and arguably just as well up-close. But the teeming four-armed shapes in the treeline eighty meters ahead, permeated Koczian with dread.

This was an alien planet. A hostile planet.

And the Fleet wanted it.

Why, she couldn't fathom. She didn't care. She was here to do a job. Half the machineheads in the galaxy were freelance mercenaries, hopping from job to job. Some were bounty hunters. Others attached themselves to contracts for the Fleet, if they had the discipline and recommendations.

Koczian had both.

She had never battled another species, though, but her wingman had.

Harry Bardoe was a decade older than her but his age had not—yet—made him the grumpy old man archetype that most crew took him for. His likeness to a heavily bearded, ungainly mountain man was too close for most people to ignore. He became the butt end of a plethora of jokes, but one reason that Koczian had managed to form a camaraderie with him so easily was his sense of humor. Well, it was dry and made landfall too rarely, but he handled mockery like a jarhead and was a true activist of the "sticks and stones" adage.

"Damn thermals are useless," Koczian sighed, toggling between an array of available imaging filters. The HUD displayed on her helmet's visor projected itself like a theater screen onto the Mech's ferroglass canopy.

She felt bad for the comparably low visibility that infantry had. Mech pilots were also elevated at least twenty feet from the ground at all times, higher depending on the model.

Harry's *Odin* was a Heavyweight, and had a particularly high cockpit, fifty feet up. He essentially sat in a window-room, the canopy surrounding him on all sides. Fortunately, it wasn't a bulbous protrusion from the top of the vaguely humanoid Mech, unlike the shoulder-mounted missile rack to his far left.

Too bad it was empty…

"Were you daydreaming during the briefing, again, K?" Harry asked.

There was that dry, barely detectable sense of humor. It carried over the private channel linked between their machines.

Koczian sighed. "No, I was just…brain-deep in the recon data."

"Always thinking about the enemy's situation, and identity. Less about their weaknesses. And strengths."

"Get off my back, old man, and stay at my heels." Koczian throttled her *Mastodon* at sixty-percent speed. The bipedal, armless Mech was stouter than Bardoe's *Odin*, but at ten tons lighter, with hocked legs, it was a touch faster on its feet.

The Mech's distinctly conical "torso" housed her cockpit, resembling the front of a passenger plane. The legs joined the sides of the torso to form its "shoulders," mounted with a missile rack each. Machineheads joked that a *Mastodon*'s racks were like its ears, as per its namesake. More akin to an actual mastodon, the Mech was fitted with two distinctly long barrels, as if horizontal tusks. Some models had these swapped for medium-bore Lasers or .50-cal machineguns, but they were typically 20mm Autocannons.

As were Koczian's.

Her missile racks were, contrarily, emptied before deployment. Bardoe wasn't thrilled about this rule, but he and his partner accepted the job with little reluctance.

At first.

"Watch your footing, K," Bardoe said, following suit. If he were to directly follow her, he would have to navigate behind the *Mastodon*. The sweeping jungle ahead of them, according to an aerial map display on their HUDs, thanks to Fleet recon, covered indeterminable acreage. This hemisphere of the planet, at least forty percent of the surface was dense jungle. Far too thick to navigate in a Mech, even a Lightweight.

Their directive as one of two dyads deployed with Gamma company was to find an alternate path into the jungle. According to aerial reconnaissance, a few shallow gullies gutted the jungle in select places, offering a possible route for Mechs.

Knowing, or at least believing, the native population to have no access to explosives or projectile weapons—except, perhaps, spears and arrows—made the contract easier to sign.

Infantry were bound to the Fleet per duty. Mech pilots, by money and agreement. Having sixty-plus tons of armor between them and the ground, and a virtually impenetrable ferroglass canopy shielding their cockpit, helped ease Koczian and Bardoe's minds.

"Still no sign of surface water," Koczian said. "What do you think it is that the Fleet wants from this place so badly?"

"Hell if I know. And we're not about to discuss it. Weapons hot, if you haven't already."

Koczian sighed. With her right thumb, she flipped the clear safety covers off the firing studs on her joystick.

"Why haven't they charged us yet?" Koczian ~~thought~~ wondered out loud.

When her wingman didn't respond right away, her left hand retracted the throttle. Stopping a sixty-ton war machine on the spot was impossible, but after a few more strides the *Mastodon* came to a halt. Twenty meters in front of it, the towering jungle trees awaited.

The canopy would clear her Mech's shoulders by about thirty feet, but would hang a mere ten feet above Bardoe's canopy.

"Harry?" Koczian asked.

She was as close to a father figure she would ever have, and although it was SOP to only use surnames, occasionally she let her heart take the helm.

Bardoe sighed, the breath carrying over their com-link in a small, calm wave of static. It wasn't any degree of anger, but deliberation.

"I don't know, K. Maybe they're studying us. People, infantry, *bodies*—that's more relatable. Approachable. But us? We're either walking monoliths to them, or two of the Four Horsemen of the Apocalypse."

Koczian snorted, shaking her head.

"What's that make me, the dreaded Pale Rider?"

"That *Mastodon* fits the bill."

Koczian smirked. He wasn't wrong.

Her Mech's legs and shoulder racks were white, or damn near. Mech bays in a deployment pod weren't known for their pristine atmosphere; grease seemed to travel in the air. After marching off the ramp when the pod made touch-down in the clearing behind them, their egg-shaped aircraft lifted off, thrusters misting their Mechs with soot.

More like *gray*, Koczian wanted to say.

The rest of the machine was painted black, giving it an odd zebra-like tone. Or a snow leopard, Koczian preferred.

Bardoe's *Odin* was aptly green and black.

Unlike infantry uniforms, it was a vibrant green. Not terribly dissimilar from the leaves and overlapping foliage they prepared to venture toward. The division of the dense jungle by this gully provided a hint of respite for the pilots' sense of security.

Theoretically, they could be ambushed from the sides, but if they moved as a column, nothing could defeat their front or rear.

Even without missiles, both Mechs offered tremendous firepower.

"Whatever the case," Koczian said, with rejuvenated commitment. "We've a mission to achieve."

"On your six, K."

It was no whimsical decision. They had run through a dozen different strategies and formational approaches before deployment. As a dyad opposed to a four-unit squad, there was only so much ground that two Mechs could cover simultaneously, especially against a seemingly endless number of unarmored personnel.

Even if they had no projectile weapons.

They were too far from the two Gamma platoons bracketing their position—First and Second—to discern their condition. The clearing they occupied was banked by hilly terrain that obstructed their view past a few hundred meters, much less a klick.

With no further information, they had to stow any complaints—or apprehension—and advance.

Bardoe took Koczian's six, trailing by a steady twenty meters.

Despite his superior height, the *Mastodon* had a broader array of weapons. The squat posture and lower perspective also allowed Koczian to observe the terrain better than Bardoe, while simultaneously keeping a vigilant eye on the jungle surrounding them.

It was evident before they even advanced that the enemy was using tree limbs and vines to navigate the jungle, as monkeys would. But shadows still teemed amid the jungle floor, too, periodically shaking a large bush in their wake.

"They're literally everywhere," she muttered. Her right forefinger hovering an inch in front of the green trigger, and her thumb five centimeters above a trio of firing studs. The biggest was red, and leftmost. The top was yellow, and the rightmost orange.

Not every pilot had their weapon groups color-coded, but it wasn't uncommon.

Which wasn't to say that she needed to glance at the joystick before firing. She could do it blindfolded, treating the studs as Braille. She wouldn't have achieved her license were she been unable to.

"Remember our mission," Bardoe said, his voice even and naturally gruff. "We aren't infantry, Ana. We infiltrate, locate, and evacuate."

Mechs couldn't traverse the jungle, not without some level of deforestation. Which the Fleet had been very clear about. So, despite their superior firepower, they were to infiltrate as a convoy of two, seek out any source of water or even a cave system, plot a waypoint, and retreat for pick-up.

Proper armored vehicles and infantry would escort exogeologists to investigate. This was the extent of their knowledge about the operation of J-726.

Characteristically, Koczian wanted to know more. And would press when she shouldn't. Bardoe wasn't alien to the urge of learning more about a mission, but he also knew better. He hated to babysit someone, and he didn't necessarily see himself as one, but part of his promise to Koczian's late brother was to "keep her on the right side of trouble."

The ex-infantry tank crewman had insisted.

"Let her annihilate trouble, and stomp it out," Erik Koczian had said. "But don't let it pull her into its depths."

That man always had a way with words.

Bardoe nodded, and shook his hand. Gave him *his* word.

Naturally, she hadn't been present for that exchange. But she wasn't dumb; she suspected something of the sort had occurred between her current wingman and her dead brother.

It wasn't even KIA.

A bar fight *after* a deployment. Erik's platoon had gone through hell for the Fleet, in the moors on Canis Nine. They stopped by at a pub on the planet Antila for celebration. A brawl erupted between civilians, and he got caught in the middle. A slip and a fall. After everything her brother had been through, a puddle of lager and leather boots dealt his fate.

If there was one promise in all his life to keep, it was the one he made with Ana's brother.

"Copy," she eventually said, clearly after bottling the urge to speak her mind.

The Fleet wasn't listening—supposedly.

"We engage if they do," Bardoe said, though he knew he didn't need to reiterate their ROE to her.

"There's just…so goddamn many of them."

She found it hard not to be in awe of the natives' sheer number, and their discipline not to attack them in an attempt to simply overrun the machines…was a bit disturbing.

"All the more to kill, when given the chance," Bardoe said.

Koczian found some solace in that bluntness. She appreciated Bardoe looking out for her, but admired his controlled bloodlust whenever she got to witness it. He was one of the most impressive Mech pilots she'd ever seen in action, and before he became freelance, he served the Fleet with accolades to prove.

"Gully's widening," she mentioned, upon realizing that their narrow path between seas of trees and thick vegetation was slowly opening up.

They were maybe two-hundred meters deep into the jungle. Had been walking for what felt like twice that, when finally the dry gully they occupied broadened into a sort of...

"I...I think it's a basin."

"No shit. How's the ground look? Coarse or soft?"

"Uh...hard to tell. Decelerating."

"Copy. Wait...hold on." Bardoe's tone sank with concern. "Lotta movement on the right. Your five."

"Are you seeing any weapons yet?"

"Handhelds, not much. Clubs mostly. Some...Some seem unarmed."

This puzzled Koczian why on Earth would a native not wield a weapon in the face of intruders?

Then it dawned on her. They weren't *on* Earth. It was just a saying, of course, but still. Something clicked in Koczian. Something Dillon once said to her. Before they separated.

"Thing is, you gotta be careful out there, ya know? I can't imagine invading another country. Or let alone, planet. I hope I never have to fight another sentient species…there's no telling how they'd act to a threat they've never seen before."

His voice, to replay it in her head, momentarily comforted her heart. But what he had said to her, it was resonating in her. Different than she'd first heard it.

"The Fleet teaches us to be smart," he had continued, and naturally she let him ramble, because every so often the man made a damn good point. "But what if the most dangerous thing is simpler than any tactic we can think up?"

Suddenly Koczian's mouth felt dry.

She eased off the throttle until the *Mastodon* came to a complete stop. Its hoof-like feet maybe three more strides from the edge of what she suspected was a drainage basin, devoid of visible water. The surrounding trees provided canopy cover over most of the clearing, which would prove why recon missed this during their fly-over last week.

Or it simply hadn't registered to them what it could be.

"K?" Bardoe asked, stopping five paces behind her. "Talk to me, what's—?"

"Reverse, Bardoe," she found her voice, hoarsely barking it out. There was a slight tremor beneath her words. "Back up, back up, back—"

Without a war cry, or a single sound, a literal *wave* of natives flung themselves off high tree branches, breaking cover and *pouring* onto the Mechs. Seven landed on the *Mastodon*, taking advantage of its broad shoulders and torso. Its lower height allowed them to land without much imbalance. Only one or two fell off, and the drop wasn't defeating. Of the ten that leapt onto the *Odin*, a mere five didn't fall.

Half of the natives in this assault wielded weapons. The others immediately began proving what Koczian had deduced from her ex-fiancé.

The simplest maneuver of all.

The least expected.

With four arms, and thus four hands, each ending in four long digits, the natives had superior purchase on the machines' many edges and nooks. With all their might, a shocking strength despite their lanky figures, the creatures began prying at whatever they could grip.

Eventually they would find the cockpit hatch, or the access panels on an armament.

She didn't know about Bardoe, but Koczian feared that their strength could override the locks on these sections in the armor.

The sheer number of them immediately concerned both pilots. Though Bardoe managed to pace back and forth a mere few steps, crushing several of the fallen natives under the seventy-ton Mech's two-toed feet, he was still overrun. Two of the eyeless, hideous-mouthed creatures stared down at him through the canopy. Both had bludgeoning weapons, striking the ferroglass with a terrifying frenzy.

"I'm only…just *starting* to get worried, here, K," he said.

"Fall back, I'm too damn close to this basin."

In spite of all their superior firepower, right now they were reduced to massive paperweights. All they could do was rotate their torsos and walk. With no arms, the *Mastodon* could jerk its torso to and fro faster than the *Odin*, but not quite sharp enough to fling any of the natives off. Their traction was too secure.

And their conviction, unwavering.

"K, you've got *two* on your left rack! Let 'em have it!"

The top quarter of each rack on the *Mastodon*'s shoulders housed a pair of medium-bore Lasers. Below them were the actual missile bays, which today were empty.

Koczian flipped a toggle on her dash, disarming her right rack, and then thumbed the firing stud for her Lasers. A green flash of light splashed the left side of her canopy, and Bardoe witnessed the Laser all but disintegrate the two natives inspecting the rack. Yellowish gore splattered that side of the Mech's torso, dripping onto the gully below. The natives' bodies, or what remained of them, slid off the rack like ragdolls.

"Got 'em," Bardoe said, backpedaling his *Odin*. "Come around, show me what I'm working with."

Aside from the two natives assailing his canopy, and a third studying the cylindrical missile rack on his

Mech's left shoulder, Bardoe was blind. His rear camera displayed nothing, so if there were more on his back, they were low.

"Copy." Koczian said, putting her back to the basin and facing her wingman. "Shit, it's bad. You've got three on the chest, one on your left leg, seems like maybe two on your ass, and—"

"I've got eyes on the others, thanks. Arms?"

"One each, but they're clear of the barrels. For now."

Koczian was surprised their animalistic curiosity had not driven them down the large-bore barrels that composed the *Odin*'s arms.

"Can you scorch 'em off?"

"You want energy, not ballistic?"

"This comes from the heart, K, but you're a much better shot with a Laser than an AC."

"Asshole," she smirked, but took it as a compliment. Universally it was much more challenging to track a small, moving target with a Laser than a ballistic weapon, especially a high-velocity Autocannon. And actually keep the three-second duration of energy *on* target.

Koczian fired her two left Lasers at the native crawling over the *Odin*'s right arm. She scorched it instantly, the two halves of its body taking a twenty-foot fall to the ground below. Then she toggled her right rack only and went to fire at the one on that arm. But it suddenly pried loose the munitions panel by the elbow, flinging the square of armor into the jungle behind it.

"Fuck, I've got an exposed ammo door!" Bardoe exclaimed, heeding the alarm on his dash.

"I can't risk it, Harry," Koczian stated the obvious, instinctively capping the firing stud with its safety cover.

"What's it doing? What's—oh, *shit*!"

Another wave of natives leapt from tree cover beside them, landing haphazardly on their Mechs.

More on Koczian's this time. Her *Mastodon* teetered to the right, as six landed on her left shoulder, two on that side of her torso. One scampered above her canopy, claws tapping the ferroglass before it began assaulting it with a clanging blade of some kind.

She cursed in Hungarian and pulled back on the throttle. The Mech reversed, extending its legs behind it just in time to keep it from falling over. Unfortunately, she knew what this meant. The ground beneath her sixty-ton machine immediately flattened. She wasn't in the gully anymore—

"Dammit, K, you've gone back too far," Bardoe snarled in frustration, struggling to keep an eye on her *Mastodon* through the swarm of enemies now crawling over his canopy. He noticed the black-and-white Mech lose elevation. His eyes widened before he shouted into his helmet's integrated mic. "You're *sinking*! Get outta there!"

Koczian throttled forward, and managed one step before alarms announced a void in balance. The Mech's gyro-core was at a loss. She felt her body slam into the back of her seat, and if it weren't for her harness she would've fallen out of it.

"They're jumping off of you! This was their goddamn plan all along!"

Koczian's view of the *Odin* began to disappear. The last thing she saw—

"Fire your left AC!" she shouted.

"Are you crazy!? The ammo door is open!"

"The dumb bastard is elbow-deep!"

Inside his cockpit, Bardoe grinned like a madman. He stuck his tongue out of his mouth in a crazed moment of bloodlust and jammed his thumb into the necessary firing stud. With his torso rotated slightly to the left, there was no risk of hitting the *Mastodon*.

The 60mm Autocannon that composed the *Odin*'s left arm fired. Two shells discharged in a flash of white fire, one after the other in rapid succession, per the weapon's design. It reloaded automatically, the next two shells chambering. This shift in the ammo bay crushed the native's arm, which had managed to hold on even through the violent vibration from the weapon's discharge.

Its body fell to the ground, and Bardoe pivoted his Mech to ensure that he stepped on its body. In the process he noticed that his stray AC had shorn a path through the canopies to his left.

"Oops," he muttered, shrugging.

All Koczian could see now, through her canopy, was sky. The planet was beautiful from a simple viewpoint. A studious gaze would prove its terror.

"Eject, K! You never liked that *mammoth* any-way!"

Koczian would have smirked or said "asshole" again if she had the morale to. Instead she confirmed the security of her harness, and reached down to grip the ejection handle between her legs. Both hands.

And up—

Through gaps in the myriad limbs of his enemy, Bardoe witnessed the *Mastodon*'s canopy pop off, in a plume of white poly-Kevlar. Koczian's ejection seat was jerked into the sky, its parachute like an artificial cloud.

He wanted to cheer, but knew that her escaping the unbalanced *Mastodon* was not a faultless life-saver. Though she had steering pulleys beneath the parachute, a strong enough gust could send her tumbling across the jungle. The chance of her penetrating the canopies if she landed on top of them was high, and after that sure death awaited.

Every pilot had a standard sidearm affixed to the side of their seat, and a Murmur SBR in a compartment behind it.

Reaching the pistol was an easy stretch.

The carbine would require a grounded landing and unharnessing from the seat.

Neither of which seemed to be in Koczian's near future.

"You read me, K!?" Bardoe yelled. He repeatedly swung his Mech's torso, successfully ridding it of one native, but the others stayed on. He could hear the canopy above him begin to crack. Tiny fissures on the exterior panels started to spider-web across the reinforced ballistic glass.

"—hear you, I—wind is—can't get to—"

Her transmission stuttering over the com-link. Bardoe's teeth grinded and he snarled through them. He turned the *Odin* to try and keep track of Koczian's ejection seat. It dangled beneath the canopy of her parachute by about eight feet.

"You're coming around, if you clear the jungle you might make the gully. I'm coming!"

He realized that what he was insinuating was ludicrous. It had been executed in training before, but deemed a last resort due to its high failure rate. In his sixteen years of experience as a Mech pilot, he had executed it once before. A second attempt resulted in the death of his wingman at the time.

That was a decade ago.

Before Koczian.

And he'd be goddamned if it happened again.

"—going—risk you—their hands—fucking crazy, Bar—"

Bardoe shook his head. He wasn't going to let her tell him what to do, or not do. Especially since he couldn't properly hear her. If they made it out of this, he'd lie and say that he had zero reception of her transmission.

Zero.

"I'm coming," he panted, throttling the *Odin* down the gully, back the way they had come.

With each stomping step that the eighty-ton machine took, Bardoe shuddered against his harness. He was no small man by any means, befitting of the *Odin*, and many would say of its namesake. The beard definitely helped.

Noticing that Koczian was airborne and out of her armored shell now, several natives began springing from the trees to flood the gully with their weapon-swinging bodies while peering up at the sky.

He wouldn't let her be captured, or even touched, by these damnable savages.

Bardoe toggled both Autocannons and snarled out loud when he thumbed the studs. The arm barrels lit up and four two-round bursts of 60mm depleted uranium shells shot downrange. Natives' bodies exploded into thick mists of green flesh and yellow gore. Divots of foliage and soil shot into the air as the shells dug their own graves.

Seconds later, he marched right over them.

Bardoe's hulking *Odin* briefly caught the shadow of Koczian's parachute as she steered it toward the gully. The biggest flaw in this plan was that the enemy currently occupied the surface of his Mech. He knew, though, that Koczian had the guts to do what she had to. Time was wasting, though. If she didn't soon—

Yellow blood splashed one of the panels of ferro-glass before him. And then another. A native tumbled off his canopy, and he spotted muzzle flashes coming

His mouth frozen open in pain and horror, his tongue lolled out of his mouth, blood framing his teeth.

The only smidgen of relief came when he saw the wounds inflicted upon the rifleman's fatal enemy. The creature's leathery green skin had been *riddled* with bullets, and the Imperator in the soldier's dead hands was not known for a lack of penetration. That wasn't all, though; the native was missing one of its lower arms, as it appeared to have been shot, messily, from its torso joint. There was also a tactical knife plunged to the hilt in its gut, which made Greenwood all the more proud of the slain soldier.

"The Fleet would be proud," he muttered. His brow furrowed, both with grief and an unparalleled anger. "Or would it?"

"Sir?" Beck had not heard him completely.

Greenwood stood up, like a rigid spring. His gaze swept the shrubland. His eyes adjusted to the sunny skies, and he spotted all of the scattered corpses, even those obscured by large leaves. So many of the enemy, so few of their own, yet the deaths had not gone easily.

"Tell the men to sort their fears," he said to Beck, passing him. A newfound vigor and fury in his voice. In his dull blue eyes. "We're taking the jungle."

Beck nodded, grimly. Resolutely.

"Yes, *sir*!"

from Koczian. She had drawn her pistol and was firing at the creatures swarming the top of his Mech.

"Atta girl!" Bardoe cheered.

He eased off the throttle, slowing the Mech to a lumbering gait.

"—hatch, I'm gonna—"

He barely caught that transmission, but didn't need to hear it again. He locked the throttle lever and disengaged decay. The Mech would continue walking forward at twenty percent speed. He twisted the center of his harness and the belts retracted. Bardoe hoisted himself to his feet, extending his arms for balance as he strode toward the back left corner of the cockpit. A retinal scan unlocked the access hatch with a pneumatic hiss.

The alarms from the dash were audible from here. Open hatch while a Mech was mobile, no good.

Bardoe flinched when he heard the ejection seat collide with the top of the *Odin*.

Outside, above the lumbering Mech, Koczian swore but counted his lucky stars that the left side, instead of the front, of her seat had not hit the *Odin*. Or else she'd have broken feet and shins. The seat clanged against the cylindrical missile rack on the *Odin*'s left shoulder.

A native sprang up from the left arm, mounting the rack and gaping its jaws up at her. In his right hand was a weapon resembling a large, iron machete. It swung it toward her, and the back of the ejection seat spewed sparks from the clash. The bottom of the seat grinded against the top of the Mech, likely jarring Bardoe's ears inside.

Finally Koczian executed the last stage of this maniacal maneuver, easily the most dreaded.

She disengaged the parachute.

The white poly-Kevlar fluttered before folding, taken by the wind.

The seat she was still harnessed to began to fall, as per the Mech's continued gait. She disengaged the harness and slid out of it seconds before the seat tumbled off the *Odin*'s back.

Inside the cockpit, Bardoe glimpsed the Mech's rear camera, in the upper right corner of his visor display. He watched the seat fall, but couldn't tell if Koczian was in it or not. His heart leapt into his throat and he lunged toward the hatch, thundering her name.

"Ana!"

Gunfire sounded.

A native fell the same way her chair had, crossing his rear camera in the blink of an eye.

Outside, Koczian was dumping rounds from her 10mm pistol left and right. Half of her attackers were losing traction in an attempt to attack her on the moving Mech, their feet not nearly as maneuverable as their hands, at least not alone.

The only reason Koczian was able stay afoot was because she wasn't. She had squatted to straddle the mound of armor between the *Odin*'s canopy and missile rack.

A sudden pain gouged her shoulder and she screamed out, dropping the pistol. It maybe had two or three rounds left in it anyway, and no extra magazines on her person.

Koczian stared up, her black ponytail whipping in the wind. The eyeless, toothy face of a J-726 native sneered down above her. It had mounted the missile rack and dug three of its four clawed digits into her left shoulder. Translucent, watery saliva spilled from the creature's mouth, dappling her Ursa Steel jumpsuit.

"Ana!" His voice caught her attention, and the native's. Its head jerked up, despite its absence of eyes.

Koczian spotted Harry Bardoe's helmeted, bearded face emerge from the open cockpit hatch. With his visor still over his visor, displaying the *Odin*'s path over his eyes, must have been madly nauseating for him.

"Full stop!" Koczian shouted.

"You're insane!"

"No, you are! Full fucking stop!"

He wouldn't battle her insistence, not given the circumstances. He returned to the heart of the cockpit, repressing the urge to draw his sidearm from the seat and go to her aid. Instead he sat down, disengaged the toggle lock, braced, and jerked it back.

Capable of stopping dead in its tracks quicker than the *Mastodon* given its straight-legged humanoid stance, the *Odin* halted a full second later.

Outside, and on top of the Mech, Koczian's breath slammed into her lungs. She felt her organs jostle as she held on, and the native's clawed fingers slip free. So did its body, tumbling off the Mech. Two of the three other natives on the *Odin*'s cockpit slipped off. One held fast, as it had noticed Bardoe likely from his voice.

Both of its upper arms snaked into the cockpit hatch, swinging its body inside.

In the ensuing stillness since the Mech came to a stop, Bardoe heard her voice shriek his name. He was relieved she had not fallen off, unless of course she was now dangling and demanding he help. Instead, when he turned toward the hatch, he came face-to-face with a native.

The whole purpose of being a Mech pilot was to put armored cushion between yourself and the enemy.

This wasn't it.

The creature's drool heralded a hissing snarl before it reached for him. Bardoe staggered back, and felt a vibration tickle his scalp, as the native's clawed fingertips scored his helmet. He collided with the cockpit seat, jarring his breath but not quite knocking it from his lungs. Keeping his gaze on the ghastly, humanoid creature as it approached him, Bardoe elbowed the compartment and it popped open.

The native lunged.

Bardoe sank to his knees, unfolding the Murmur's buttstock and burying it into his hip. Safety off, by default. He squeezed the trigger, and a spray of bullets hosed into the creature's chest. He elevated his aim, as its towering body persisted. In the blink of an eye, a dozen 5.56mm bullets scattered its brain across the ceiling of the cockpit.

The creature flopped over in a heap.

Koczian appeared in the access hatch, limping and grasping a shoulder wound. Bardoe spotted red streaks through her fingers. He hoisted himself afoot, dropping the SBR, and stumbled over the slain native. He put one hand on her good shoulder, and then reached past, closing the hatch. Its magnetic locks clanged in place.

Fresh alarms sounded. Another munitions panel had been torn free. And the canopy integrity was at sixty percent. Not a horrible number, but considering they had achieved it with clubs and machetes alone was unnerving.

"You good?" Bardoe asked.

She mustered a nod, wide-eyed. "You?"

"Gonna have one helluva bruise tomorrow, tell ya what," he said wryly, and returned to his seat.

Koczian shook her head, and meandered toward the seat. She grimaced at the dead native on the floor, between his seat and the access hatch, a twelve-foot stretch. Part of her feared it wasn't dead, and hated turning her back on it.

"I'm here," she said. "Full throttle."

"Yes, ma'am."

After all of that, he wasn't about to second-guess her. He secured his harness and slowly pushed the throttle forward.

The *Odin* resumed its march, sluggishly gaining speed. The rocking cockpit nearly made Koczian lose her footing, but she held onto the seat steadfast. The pain in her shoulder doubled, but she didn't let go.

Once clear of the gully, the natives ceased attacking the Mech. He turned it around, never easing off the throttle until a full crescent had been performed, and once more faced the jungle.

Those not still between the seas of trees continued to charge the Mech, while the others retreated into the jungle.

Bardoe opened fire, sweeping his arms to stagger the two-round bursts. Four 60mm AC shells shattered seven bodies and devoured yellow-sprayed shrubbery.

He centered the *Odin*'s torso and surveyed the scene. Not a single one twitched. Silhouettes lingered amid the treelines, and beneath high canopies. Watching him. Studying the machine, perhaps not with their eyeless faces, but some other form of perception.

Neither of the pilots could fathom how.

Neither of them wanted to.

For the first time in her life, Ana Koczian didn't care to learn more.

She wanted off this rock, and prayed that the bulk of infantry survived to see the stars again, too.

3

They were never at risk of losing daylight. However, Gamma company had not accounted for this level of tree cover. The jungle canopy was a thicket of overlapping branches, leaves, and vines. Lower boughs a mere few feet above the soldiers' heads were densely vegetated and underbrush in the jungle was too thick to easily navigate.

Having pushed through at a cautious pace for the past ten minutes, time passing like a slug in tar, at least nobody had encountered a dangerous plant. No thorns or fly traps. Nothing toxic, although there was no telling what might happen if something was eaten.

Most of the foliage was green. Variations in color of the flora were low. Except—

An occasional splash of yellow on a leaf indicated a wounded enemy, slinking through the jungle in retreat. The question of a possible trap or ambush had been raised among the remains of First Platoon, which Greenwood openly admitted was possible.

Beck didn't like hearing this level of honesty, but perhaps it was best for their men to know the risk. Perhaps their own fear could be used as a weapon of determination.

The Gunnery Sergeant's speech before they penetrated the treeline had stirred the previously stalled hearts of many. Had it been particularly livening, or inadvertently demoralizing? To know that their CO was pushing them into the bosom of the enemy's stronghold?

Most of the platoon kept quiet and complied.

Orders were orders, and this was their mission.

Badge found it oddly convincing of their strength as a unit. Their losses in the tallgrass were nil; he was relieved to see Holloway still sucking air. The young man was rattled, but hanging on. And their losses in the shrubland had been rough, but at good odds.

He hated to look at casualties as mere statistics, but it helped him survive the horror of it.

Beneath the canopy, their visibility was hindered. Grenadiers had been positioned at the outset of their fanned formation, and harbored the most fear, despite their firepower, of being picked off by the skulking enemy. Medics, toward the rear but in front of their CO, dreaded being plucked from above.

Beck led at point.

Greenwood's head was on a constant swivel, sometimes his whole body, as he held the rear.

Badge and McLeod trudged beside each other, two cubits apart. Except for Beck, ahead of them, nobody was downrange. Behind them, the platoon's two medics and their CO. Badge knew Holloway was somewhere left of him, and Araújo to McLeod's far right.

He periodically glanced at the compass display on his visor, keeping note of the Lieutenant's position. Whereas Beck was visible, almost at all times. Except when Badge had to push past a huge bush or a leaf nearly the size of a man.

He tried to ignore the paranoia he had of seeing Beck ten paces ahead of him one second, and gone the next, without a sound.

Naturally, Badge couldn't fathom a man, or soldier, like Beck, being attacked and not making a peep. Even if his throat was cut, if his head was still attached, the Gunnery Sergeant would make damn sure everyone in the entire jungle knew about it.

Seconds after fusing this thought, and burying the ones questioning why their abundant enemy had not yet attacked them, Beck raised his right fist. It cleared a nearby fern and most of the platoon took notice, stopping in their tracks.

"What've you got, Beck?" Greenwood asked, via their private com-link.

"Hard to say. Can't see a damn thing down here." He paused, wiped his mouth with a knuckle, and sighed before replying, more sternly. "Two o'clock, movement."

"Elaborate."

"A big ass leaf is swaying." A brief pause. "Sir, I don't think it was the wind."

"No shit," Greenwood muttered, without transmitting the reply.

He looked up. No wind could penetrate these canopies, and they were too far from the treeline now to feel any version of a gust.

"I'm pulling a grenadier to your far right," he transmitted. "Put one on you, vanguard, advance—your eleven. Slowly."

"Copy." Beck removed his hand from the helmet, and then put it into the air, tucking his thumb inward to form a 'G.' Followed by a raised index finger, and then his hand became uniform, fingers out, and he waved it toward his eleven o'clock.

One of the grenadiers behind him bent his knees and hustled forward. Thick leaves and other flora slapped at his body as he advanced, the only sound currently permeating the jungle.

They had it on good merit that the enemy possessed a superior sense of hearing, given their eyeless faces. It was theorized that they could smell like a wolf, too, if not better—despite an absence of visible nostrils. Nothing about the creatures made much sense.

Better safe than sorry...

Until now, since entering the jungle, Beck had exchanged his Reaper for the Cutter. Though not integrally suppressed like the Murmur that some of the men carried, the Cutter's reports were significantly quieter than the assault shotgun. The bayonet, however proven ineffectual against the natives, at least provided a hint of close-quarters comfort in the Reaper's absence.

Worst-case, Beck figured, he could rip one of their hands off with his bare hands. More an exaggeration to boost his morale than true faith, but anything was possible on J-726.

"How do you think the other platoons are faring?" Holloway asked the soldier beside him. Badge heard his voice, just barely, a hushed whisper that still carried with it the loudness of paranoia.

"Same as us, I reckon," the infantryman beside him answered, with an Alabama twang. A tank of a man, naturally a grenadier, who regretted not moving sooner and being the one to join their XO.

Frank Cudlitz was the only man in First Platoon that gave Beck a run for his money in the scary factor. It was more his *ability* to be intimidating, besides his sheer size, than his demeanor. More often than not, Cudlitz was a gentle giant.

Until he put his training to work.

"Keep it down, fuck's sake!" another soldier spat, under his breath, nearly on the other side of the for-mation.

Behind the fanned-out men, their arrangement like a broad arrow, Greenwood merely shook his head.

He was, at this point, moving as planned. A gren-adier followed suit, Enrico Silva. Not as much brawn as Cudlitz or most grenadiers, but he'd excelled at boot and proven many wrong.

Greenwood was confident having him at his heels.

Ahead of Beck, he spotted another sign of move-ment. This time, a bush composed of smaller leaves and protruding, tubular red flowers, shuddered. Too fresh to have been in the wake of something long gone.

He gestured, and his attached grenadier shouldered the Thunder LMG more attentively.

A flurry of leaves and twigs showered both of them from above. A hiss punctuated the attack, but not the shrill shriek that Beck imagined in his mind. The quietness of their enemy had still been most unnerving.

A lanky native descended, one of its hands clutching a lower branch to support it as it dangled. A machete swung, cutting air and flesh just as easily. Beck had turned and hunkered down simultaneously, just in time to witness the grenadier's head be lopped off. It was so close to Beck that the poor soldier's blood misted his cheeks.

Something in Beck let loose, a nut or bolt or every leash to every dog.

"Motherfucker!" he roared, firing his Cutter up at the enemy. Bullets shredded skin and peppered branches. The native managed to swing itself free of his line-of-fire, dripping small beads of yellow blood onto his visor and shoulders.

As he rolled through a lush fern, Beck heard scattered gunfire from the platoon behind him. He came up on a knee, still low, and wiped his visor with a sleeve. The alien blood smeared and made his visor opaque. He cursed under his breath and raised it, helmet still on.

"*Trees*!" someone bellowed, a baritone vaulting above their heads. "They're in the *trees*!"

Greenwood witnessed it from a farther back position. He and Silva gawked up. Thinner branches shuddered as natives leapt to and fro. Leaves fluttered down, amid smaller twigs snapping beneath the creatures' transferred weight.

"Open fire, Gamma!"

Their CO's voice was unmistakable. It was a shame that the other platoons, kilometers away, couldn't hear him. Some of the men wondered how *they* were faring, and with less distinct officers. Making this platoon, or what remained of them, especially grateful.

For what it was worth.

"Get low and light 'em up!" Greenwood added.

The already spread-out infantrymen hunkered down and aimed skyward, only the occasional beam of sunlight piercing the canopy providing a glimpse of visibility. Within seconds, some of the men were inadvertently marking targets via their optics and visors. This helped, but the mobility of the red-haloed natives was dizzying.

"You heard the LT!" Beck hollered, regaining his wherewithal as a soldier, moreover an XO. No better way than to lead by example, throwing his voice into the air like rolling thunder, as the muzzle of his weapon lit up one burst at a time. "Make four arms no arms, stagnant water is as good as a puddle o' blood!"

Badge shook his head, and would have cracked a smirk had the circumstances permitted.

Since the first spurt of gunfire ahead of him, their enemy was coming out of the woodwork. Almost literally. They descended from above, sometimes seeming to materialize out of thin air. In reality their green coloration and lanky figures in the poorly illuminated environment made them nearly invisible to the soldiers below.

Nearing his first reload, Badge felt the rifleman to his right nudge him. Forcefully. Badge nearly lost his balance, and began to curse at the man when he noticed his comrade was headless. An arterial spurt from one of his severed carotids coated Badge's left shoulder with blood. The warmth made his underlying skin crawl, and an inescapable nausea struck him almost as hard as the dead soldier's body had.

Unable to find his voice and scream as per impulse, Badge instead teetered onto his right side and fumbled with his weapon.

Above him, likely the cause of the decapitation, a native swung. Its four-foot iron-like machete sundered a huge leaf by Badge's head, and even over the sputtering gunfire around him, much less his own hammering heart, he could still hear the *whoosh* of air. Inches from his face.

Badge rolled twice, and it would have been three but he knocked against another rifleman. He was *sitting* on the jungle floor, which Badge couldn't understand. At first. Then he pulled himself up, and realized why the man sat with his legs extended. His throat had been cleaved, and his spinal column severed. His jugular a gaping scarlet wound, and a sight that Badge knew would stick with him for the rest of his natural life. Worse, the slain soldier's head dangled between his shoulder blades. The only reason the corpse was propped upright was because a bullet-riddled native had fallen in a heap on the man's right side.

Moments after Badge sucked in a rancid breath to formulate a gasp, and recoiled, his contact with the body, however slight, made it fall over.

The gung-ho motivation he had reeled in earlier was now evaporating before his very eyes.

"Say it sucks for him," came a familiar, Scottish voice. And then a vice grip on his shoulder, nearly hoisting Badge to his feet all on his own.

McLeod came into view, crouching beside Badge as his hands shook their way through a reload.

"Or that he's better off, not being in this shit," the PFC added. He shrugged, brandishing his pistol and racking the slide to check the chamber. "Either way, decide fast and move on. The boys need you."

Badge gulped and found it within himself not to let fear devour him.

Then his brow furrowed as he looked over McLeod. There was blood splatter on his uniform, both red and yellow.

"Not mine," he said, reading Badge's gaze. Then he shook his head, his own eyes desultory for a moment. "Hodgson took a club to the dome. I've never seen a man's skull cave like that before."

Badge gulped, and mentally fought past that image. When he looked over his shoulder, a native, likely the one that had taken a swing at him earlier—*thirty seconds ago? sixty? what was time anymore?* —was monkey-swinging toward them.

A grenadier's stream of high-caliber fire literally cut it in half at the waist. The two pieces tumbled through the air, a loop of vines catching the legs while the torso crashed into a shrub.

Badge's gaze returned to McLeod, in time to see him pump six fast rounds from his pistol into a native that was on the ground. Crawling toward them like a spider, parting foliage in its wake. At least three of his bullets penetrated its skull, rendering it limp.

Relieved to see some degree of mortality in the enemy, Badge was hoisted from his slump.

"Where's your rifle?" he asked.

"Oh, uh, dropped it…back, uh…I don't know, fuckin' somewhere."

"Take mine, too," Badge offered his own pistol.

"Appreciate it, but no. Besides, Beck would chew my ass out if he knew I bereaved you of your *Fleet-issue* sidearm."

The iota of sarcasm in McLeod's voice was something that Badge had to cherish.

And then a shriek cut through their ranks.

It wasn't just a scream, it was an effete wail saturated with pain. Behind Badge and McLeod, one of the medics had been hunkered over Holloway, whose arm was missing at the shoulder. A consistent jet of blood painted nearby underbrush, the medic struggling to treat the wound. His determination was admirable, until nullified by a swinging native that knocked him back. The native landed and plunged its blade into the medic's chest, just as he rose up on his knees.

Behind the poor soul, whose name he didn't know from this angle, but suspected it was Earl Delaney, Greenwood watched in horror. The medic's back, between his shoulder blades, erupted in a spray of blood as the enemy's blade punched through. Greenwood was mid-reload, but the sight shook even his veteran hands to drop his magazine. He proceeded to fumble for it in the heavy vegetation, a blood-soaked leaf sliming across his face and violating his senses.

Milliseconds before he slammed the fresh mag home, Silva stepped forward and laid down a burst from his LMG. From chest to neck, the native exploded in a plume of yellow gore. Its head bobbed through some ferns to Silva's right, while the rest of its body slumped to the left of the slain medic.

His harrowing scream at the foot of death's door was the last thing to have come out of his mouth.

Silva moved on, continuing to burst-fire his machinegun at natives swinging from the trees and lashing out with their bladed weapons.

Behind him, now by some twenty paces, Lieutenant Greenwood crawled toward the medic's body. It *was* Delaney, one of the most committed medics he had ever had the honor of overseeing.

His heart sank a little more than it had already, and an ire bubbled in his veins.

Greenwood hoisted himself up and attempted to survey the status of his platoon, scattered out ahead of him. According to his visor, Beck was eighteen meters away, at his one o'clock. His eyes provided little respite, for what he *could* see was simply disheartening.

Bodies. Too many of them First Platoon, and not enough of the enemy.

The only crumb of relief came when he realized that the natives—more than half whose heads were marked with red rings in his visor—were retreating. Ascending higher into the trees, swinging or leaping farther and farther away. In virtually every direction it seemed.

Ten seconds later, all gunfire ceased, and Greenwood could hear scattered groans of pain in the jungle.

"Cluster, cluster!" He shouted, wading through the underbrush while standing straight up. "Check your ammo, tend to wounds! Delaney is KIA, where is Warner!?"

Travis Warner, their other medic.

Greenwood prayed the man was still alive.

Far ahead of him, though the Lieutenant was trying to close that distance, Beck called out.

"Grenadiers, sound off!"

Gradually, the surviving grenadiers announced themselves. To Greenwood's displeasure, only two seemed to have survived the encounter.

Silva, at his three o'clock kneeling beside a tree and reloading, and Cudlitz, ten paces to his left, helping a wounded rifleman.

"Warner, goddammit, sound off!" Greenwood shouted.

Almost interrupting him, someone exclaimed a series of words that the CO had been dreading.

"Travis is gone, sir! He's fucking *dead*!"

The pain in the soldier's voice was palpable even from afar. Greenwood stopped walking, and tried to locate its source.

Audible sniffling in the comparable silence now coating the jungle was easy to track down.

He recognized Private Araújo, who had been scored down the back by an enemy weapon, and tended to by another rifleman. The blood seeping through the broad gash, staining his sliced uniform, was troubling. That Araújo had not passed out yet was both admirable and unnerving.

"Corporal," Greenwood said, hunkering down beside McLeod. He grimaced at the sight of Araújo's wound, and squeezed his bicep in comfort. "How's he looking?"

"I'm no medic, sir, but it ain't as deep as it looks. Just trying to clean the wound, get it packed with some gauze from Warner's kit, and—"

McLeod was interrupted.

Beck, ahead. Comfortably closer than before. Instead of using their com-link, he addressed his CO in the open.

"LT! You need to see this."

"What is it, Beck?" Greenwood began to stand. His left hand went from the trembling Araújo to the dedicatedly firm McLeod, and then lifted.

Beck was about fifteen feet away, and coming closer. Panting, and sporting a gouge in the shoulder, perhaps from a claw, but not too severe. Otherwise, he appeared unwounded.

Physically, anyway.

"A clearing, I think. Fifty, sixty meters. Picked up an Imperator, the optic seems to be telling the truth."

Greenwood nodded. He looked around.

"Good, we could use a breath of fresh air." He didn't even want to utter out loud their head count. It was now just barely in the single digits. "Whose rifle did you borrow?"

"Not borrow, sir. Unfortunately, he won't be needing it anymore."

"Goddammit," Greenwood muttered.

"Sir, can I help?" A deep voice over his right shoulder. Greenwood turned to see Silva standing at attention. Sweat, dirt, and blood—both colors—tarnishing his already dark complexion. "We have more casualties than wounded. I'd like to volunteer as a scouting party for the clearing that the XO mentioned. Sir."

Greenwood nodded.

"I appreciate your courage, PSC. What do you think, Beck?"

"Sooner than later. Three's a party, though."

Greenwood looked around and gestured. The remains of his men had gathered into two clusters of three. The eight of them occupied a twenty-foot radius in the jungle.

"Corporal," he gestured at McLeod. The soldier patted Araújo's back, muttered something into his ear, and stood up, approaching the Lieutenant. Then Greenwood whistled at two riflemen exchanging words in private.

But Beck interrupted, stepping forward.

"Sir, allow me."

"Beck, I can't risk—"

"Neither my rank nor my experience puts me above any man here," Beck stated, with such firmness that his declaration reached every soul present. Greenwood saw more humanity in the XO's eyes in this moment than ever before, and he had served with the Gunnery Sergeant since his retirement as a machinehead. And then Beck added: "Not even Private Holloway back there."

Greenwood glanced over his shoulder.

Holloway, whose shoulder wound Delaney had been treating, was either unconscious or dead. Still, his immobile right hand had clutched the sleeve of Delaney's uniform. And still held on.

Greenwood gathered a deep, haggard breath.

"Retrieve your Reaper, and advance."

Beck's chin lifted. "With caution or urgency, sir?"

"A grave deal of both, if you can manage, Gunnery Sergeant."

"Yes, sir!" Beck damn near shouted. Then he relaxed a little, and began to turn. He gestured at McLeod and Silva. "On me, gentlemen."

Some twelve feet to Greenwood's right, Badge exchanged fleeting eye contact with McLeod. A subtle nod was thrown his way, and much like his bite of sarcasm earlier, Badge would cherish it.

The rifleman whose company he shared was a peculiar Jamie Tristan. The Private was a thoroughbred smart-ass if ever there was one, and a chatterbox that made him a royal pain-in-the-ass under virtually any circumstance.

He had managed to evade Badge's radar until the end of this recent debacle. Now he felt glued to the young man, which Badge felt bittersweet about. On one hand, Tristan's rants were a glimpse of humanity that, while a bit looney, were still vaguely comforting considering their circumstances. On another, Tristan's cynicism was especially demoralizing, perhaps getting under Badge's skin more easily than most.

Greenwood moved around, checking on his men. After having a word with Araújo, he moved over to Cudlitz, while Tristan talked off Badge's ear even as he avoided eye contact.

Badge went from watching his CO to spotting the silhouettes of Beck, McLeod, and Silva get farther and farther away from them. The clearing ahead was only visible when Badge peered downrange via the optic on his Imperator. Even this motion didn't put a hitch in Tristan's voice.

Badge sighed, lowering his rifle.

Finally, he made his senses vulnerable to Tristan's rambling.

"I mean, clearly the Fleet gives far less shits about their own infantry than they do their *precious* machine-heads."

Thinking of Ana, Badge deflected.

"It isn't like they don't have their merits."

"Struck a nerve, did I?"

Badge rolled his eyes.

"I'm just saying…" he continued on, not waning even as Greenwood circled around toward them. Their CO redirected to Holloway, likely to check his pulse and confirm his condition. The next time Badge tuned Tristan's voice back on, he was going off about their purpose on Jade. "The fuck are we even doing here? I mean, what's so special about these damn things?"

Sitting on his ass to nobody's surprise, Tristan kicked the base of a tree.

"*Harvest*, yeah right. The only thing they're gonna harvest from this big green rock is—"

The word "death" never fully escaped his mouth. A native abruptly leapt from the underbrush behind him, making hardly a sound. It tackled the unsuspecting Tristan within arm's reach of Badge, and they tumbled in a mess of limbs before crashing into a patch of shrubs.

A mere ten feet away when it happened, Greenwood was nearly startled out of his boots. He fumbled with his weapon, hanging on his shoulder by its sling. The soldiers behind him jolted to attention, even Araújo, at the sound of the tussle.

Despite the height of a native, it had vanished, with Tristan, below the dense foliage, out of everyone's line-of-sight. Even the standing Greenwood. Then a giant fern shuddered, and a burst of screaming cut off as quickly as it had erupted.

Everyone was on their feet now, weapons wielded.

Greenwood and Badge both flinched at the sound of something snapping, then ripping, and a thick mist of blood painted the ferns.

"R and R is over, gentlemen," Greenwood muttered, barely audible. Then his voice climbed. "Badge, you're on point. To the clearing, everyone, go, *now!*"

The men gathered, Badge leading. There was a tentativeness to his gait, but it swiftly dissolved when more natives sprung from hiding. They seemed to come from all angles, and on the jungle floor, not above. Which meant they had been there all along, during the infantry's respite, *waiting*. Or, they'd been crawling, methodically patient and slowly, inward.

Either way, this realization was especially jarring. For Badge, motivating.

"On me, on me, on me!" he shouted repeatedly, slapping the top of his helmet and vaulting over a smaller bush here and there. He gave Jamie Tristan a wide berth, subconsciously wishing he had bantered with him. After passing the site, Tristan's killer popped up from the bloody foliage like a jack-in-the-box. Its four hands were empty, except for the rags of flesh hanging from its claws.

Badge didn't see this, his gaze was set on the clearing sixty meters out. The thick vegetation and low-hanging vines toward the treeline made it hard to gauge distance.

Behind him, Greenwood sized up the enemy staring in Badge's direction, and opened fire. His Imperator drove a few rounds into the side of the creature's skull, or so he would've liked to believe. At least two hit their mark, making the native's head bob to the right before its body slinked into the foliage and vanished.

Greenwood cursed through gritted teeth.

Behind him, Cudlitz helped Araújo forward.

Their CO gathered his breath and headed in the opposite direction, his studious gaze eventually finding Holloway in the mess of dimly lit undergrowth. When he hunkered down beside the man, his gaping shoulder wound dressed but soaked through, Greenwood slid a finger under the man's jaw. Holloway's skin was paler than death, and beads of sweat covered him like Braille.

Greenwood's lips formed profanity but his voice didn't pass clenched teeth.

A sadness dripped from him and he shed it as quickly as only a man of his rank could. Then he returned to his feet and began to follow his men toward the clearing. Periodically he paused to fire his Imperator in either direction, left and right, whenever a hint of motion caught his eye.

Lieutenant Greenwood couldn't help but feel like they were being *herded* toward the clearing.

Given his experience under the jungle canopy, he suddenly didn't care.

Dying under a clear sky was always better than any alternative. Beck had told him this, during their second month together. Back when Greenwood was a Corporal.

About forty meters ahead of the Lieutenant, the ragtag remains of First Platoon were in the open. The clearing was a meager forty meters across, at its widest, an oval shape. Fifty paces from where Badge and the others emerged, McLeod and Silva knelt. They were investigating a jagged fissure in the ground, where a smooth convex structure of rock emerged slightly from the surrounding grass. They looked up from where they knelt, to watch their XO greet the other infantrymen.

Beck helped Cudlitz with Araújo, who was proving more capable on his own despite his wound. Badge caught his breath, and made brief eye contact with McLeod. Unlike the last time, there was now a sullen gravity to Badge's expression, which McLeod picked up on with ease.

Naturally, they had heard the gunfire preceding the men's emergence from the treeline.

"Where's LT?" Beck demanded.

"He's coming," Cudlitz said, turning away from Araújo, who Silva now helped, to step back into the treeline. Cudlitz shouldered his Thunder and peered downrange. The frameless, projected red-dot optic became his best friend. He lined up a pair of targets emerging from the underbrush to Greenwood's far right, which the Lieutenant didn't seem to notice.

Beck started to say something, when Cudlitz let it rip. Tight bursts put the creatures out of commission at thirty meters, shredding foliage in the process.

Greenwood flinched but kept running.

He had about reached the treeline when Beck stepped back under the canopy to welcome his CO, and a native swung down from above. Two flat feet struck Beck in the chest, vaulting him back. Head over heels he tumbled, blood sputtering from his mouth. A rib had broken, and punctured his right lung.

"Fuck!" Silva exclaimed, leaving Araújo to help Beck. He paused to open fire on the charging native, which didn't have a weapon in any of its hands. Silva cut the creature into thirds with a hose of .308 Magnum rounds. Beck rose to a knee, teetering, and worked his Reaper back into the ready position. Blood frothed through his lips, sticking to the white stubble on his chin.

Silva went to his aid, while Cudlitz escorted Greenwood into the clearing. He sporadically paused to fire bursts back into the jungle.

"Holloway?" McLeod asked Badge, as he strode toward their XO.

Badge grimly shook his head.

McLeod processed it on the run. As he reached the others, a blur of movement spun him around.

"Contact, four o'clock!" he hollered, shouldering the Imperator and firing.

A swarm of natives had emerged from the treeline thirty paces from Araújo. Two skittered left and right, avoiding McLeod's precision marksmanship. A third took several rounds from Badge, at a better angle, as it neared Araújo. The wounded man was kneeling and firing his suppressed SBR at the encroaching enemy. Even as bullets cut through the creature's lanky form, from two directions, it managed to swing the machete with incredible reach.

Araújo's lower jaw disintegrated against the force, his cheeks bisected and his tongue falling with the severed mandible. Blood and saliva poured from his mouth, the ability to scream failing him.

Badge screamed and advanced.

McLeod finally put down one of the natives, but the second had reached him, minimally wounded. It swung a club at him from his left, and he ducked it, rolling back. He shed his Imperator as it was empty and he had no time to reload. His pistol came up in both hands, barking out round after round into the creature's midsection.

Silva provided supportive fire, skirting to the left for a better angle.

Cudlitz would have helped but was engaging the enemy at the treeline, backing away from it but unable to safely turn away.

Beck finally forced himself afoot, pushing Greenwood's arms away, and as more natives poured from the treeline in front of Badge and McLeod, he rushed with his Reaper hipped. The assault shotgun's drum cycled as shells pumped out at an alarming rate. If the enemy didn't know fear, they began to develop it when their bodies grew nasty craters or limbs were blown off as Beck approached. He screamed and roared with pain and rage as he got nearer, the Reaper faithful to its name.

"Reloading!" Badge announced, dropping to a knee where grass met rock.

McLeod dumped the remainder of his pistol magazine into a native approaching Badge. Its left arm went limp just in time, and it dropped the club it was wielding. Badge felt relieved as he finalized his reload, but suddenly another native charged in its place.

"Fall back!" Greenwood shouted, releasing concise yet tentative bursts from his assault rifle, paranoid of friendly fire.

Beck had annihilated five enemies in the span of ten seconds by the time his drum went dry and two flanked Cudlitz to leap at him from the treeline.

Silva aided Badge, pushing forward with his LMG opening up.

"Patton!" Greenwood shouted, his voice straining. None of the men in the clearing had ever heard their CO call Beck by his first name, in their presence anyway.

The Reaper was thrown from Beck's hands by a swinging club, which then came back around to wallop the Gunnery Sergeant in the ribs. The same side already injured. Beck practically flew through the air, landed hard where grass met rock, and rolled into Araújo.

A native had stepped over the severely wounded Araújo to approach Badge and Silva, facing a wave of bullets as if trying to die. And then Silva's LMG went dry, and he knew that reloading the belt-fed weapon meant death in these circumstances.

So he dropped the weapon with a loud clatter, unslung his Cutter, and instead of firing it, charged the creature.

With a final blood-clogged breath, Edwin Araújo reached out to grab the native's left ankle. The drab green skin was simultaneously coarse and smooth, like damp rawhide. Despite facing the Light at the end of the Tunnel behind his eyes, Araújo held on.

The native hissed through haphazardly arranged teeth and glanced back down at the human giving it pause.

Then Silva arrived, plunging the seven-inch serrated bayonet on his weapon into the base of the creature's gut. Badge watched in awe, dreading a repetition of the first sight he had beheld today. He was in the throes of clearing a jammed breech with his Imperator, when he looked up and a little victory reared its face—

Silva yanked the Cutter skyward, splitting the sexless native from groin to throat. Viscera poured forth, some of it gray and pink but most of it a sallow color, drenching the Cutter and the big hands that held it. Silva released an animalistic cry that was part growl, part roar, and part scream, as he sawed the serrated blade as high as it would go. The native shuddered repeatedly before staggering back, all but emptied.

Araújo was lucky to have not been bathed in any of the gore, before the life evacuated him entirely.

Greenwood, meanwhile, had managed to kill Beck's attacker, and suppressed another back into the jungle. Cudlitz was returning to the group, risking a mobile reload.

McLeod helped Badge to his feet, who finally cleared the jam of a casing lodged into the Imperator's breech. He began to thank McLeod but instead violently shoved him in the chest. From the right corner of his eye, he had glimpsed movement. A native had flanked them, in the open while everyone else was busy—or dead—and taken a swing at McLeod.

The machete cut only air thanks to Badge's impulsive reaction.

Unfortunately, the PFC's boot heel caught the lip of the fissure he had been peering into earlier, and he fell back. Badge dumped a curt four-round burst into the native's gut as he ducked and dove for McLeod. The soldier's shoulder blades struck the other end of the slit in the rock, and he folded inward, falling into the abyss below.

Badge had managed to grab an ankle before he hit the ground, but McLeod's plunging momentum couldn't be saved. The rock surface was slick, almost moist. Badge's free hand slid free from the Imperator in a last-ditch attempt to grab the edge of the hole as he went in, headfirst.

No traction.

Badge and McLeod plummeted into the cavernous belly of J-726.

Their reactive cries echoed, almost failing to reach the surface.

Topside, Silva stood up from Araújo, burying his grief. But beyond proud of the soldier for his final efforts of courage and camaraderie.

He had not heard Badge and McLeod's voices, but their sudden disappearance, and his recent memory of inspecting the hole in the rock with the PFC, drove him toward it.

Behind him, Sean Greenwood watched, and felt, Patton Beck's weathered hand loosen in his own. Though the parameters were beyond reasonable, and he held nothing against the man, Cudlitz swore to himself that he would never admit to anyone that he saw *the* Lieutenant Greenwood shed tears. Much less over the death of another man, but of course, Cudlitz wasn't oblivious to the fact that he and Beck were more than brothers-in-arms.

They had been friends.

Thirty feet away, Silva whistled. When Greenwood and Cudlitz looked up, they saw the grenadier beckon them. They exchanged looks, nodded grimly, and then hustled to regroup.

"I think McLeod and Badge took a fall," Silva said, his deep voice tinged with grief.

"We're not dead yet, for fuck's sake!" McLeod's distinctive voice barely reached them.

Silva's head bowed, and he chanced a smirk, before shaking it. Greenwood's right hand slapped Silva's broad shoulder, squeezing it. Silva looked up and they exchanged relieved expressions.

"I'm gonna gather some vines," Cudlitz said, still carrying his freshly reloaded LMG.

"Sharp man," Greenwood said. He gestured with his head, at Silva. "Give him a hand, and a second pair of eyes. I'll be goddamned if I lose anyone else, much less the best fucking grenadiers I've ever fought beside."

Silva nodded firmly. There was tacit appreciation in his dark brown eyes.

"You got it, sir." Then he leaned down, and cupped his hands over his mouth. "Back soon, fellas!"

Immediately, both Badge and McLeod's voices were overlapping, shouting things like "don't you fucking leave us" and "get your fat ass back here!" Greenwood couldn't resist smiling, and given recent tragedies—this whole deployment was one big clusterfuck—he had to appreciate lighter moments.

However small by comparison.

"This is your CO! I'm right here!" Greenwood shouted down into the fissure. He was kneeling, uncomfortably, on the rock. But he wanted to be as close as possible to his men, who he couldn't see at all. Despite being beneath unobstructed, clear skies and a sun that wouldn't see nightfall for another few hours, it was pure blackness below.

"Happy to hear your voice, sir!" McLeod replied.

"Talk to me, fellas! What's your condition?"

"We're good, we're alive!" McLeod shouted.

"No injuries, sir!" Badge added.

"Just some major bruising, nothing to write home about!" McLeod admitted.

Greenwood nodded. "That's great news! Listen, we're working on getting you boys outta there, pronto."

He looked over his shoulder and saw Cudlitz looping thick, dark green vines around his hand and elbow. Meanwhile, Silva vigilantly surveyed the surrounding jungle.

"Can't fuckin' wait, Lieutenant!" Badge responded.

Greenwood smirked, ever so briefly. Then, he finally let his curiosity crawl out, as he couldn't resist the question.

"Any water down there?"

A touch of joy, for lack of a better word, in McLeod's voice.

"If there wasn't, we'd be dead, sir! It's a helluva drop!"

Greenwood shook his head, that smirk taking up residence on his face. He wished Beck was here to hear it, even if finding a water source wasn't their mission, he knew it would bring good tidings for his Fleet superiors. Despite the horrors they had witnessed, and endured, the deaths and likely trauma many of the men would be leaving with.

Supposing any of them actually make it off-planet.

"Copy that, Sergeant!" Greenwood called down. "Now just hang tight."

A few seconds passed.

"Uh, sir!" McLeod. "It's Corporal!"

"Not anymore, Trevor. You boys stay put, don't go for a swim or anything, and before you know it we'll all be drinking to Beck's memory in a pub on Antila!"

Of course, Greenwood had not forgotten the names—and faces, god, their *faces*—of everyone else in his platoon that he had lost today. From Araújo to Holloway to the many dead they had to leave in the field before they ever ventured into the jungle.

Despite his insinuation of Beck's death, Greenwood thought he heard a chuckle from the darkness below. He imagined the two infantrymen gathering their wits in lieu of the bad news, and trying to appreciate the good. The bright side was virtually imperceptible after experiencing literal hell, and for no known reason.

Greenwood remained at a loss as to *why* the Fleet had its heart set on this godforsaken planet. Proof that looks weren't everything.

"Sir! Private Badge here!"

"Loud and clear, soldier. What can I do for you?"

He imagined the all-too-humble Dillon Badge smirking before answering, his voice growing dryer by the second, and perceptibly exhausted. Yet, still dedicated to keeping this line of communications open.

And, apparently, bolstering their morale.

"Any chance we can make that Brosia, Lieutenant? I hear their vodka is as crisp and persuasive as the clear sea itself!"

Greenwood, once more, couldn't resist a smirk. He shook his head, and peripherally noticed Cudlitz approaching. A quick glance confirmed that Silva trailed him, still attentive of the surrounding treeline.

Looking back down into the darkness, Greenwood responded with a faint air of enthusiasm.

"We can negotiate later, Private! I'm sure the other platoons will want a say!"

All he could think of, then, was the condition of his other men, what felt like leagues away, and the pending deployment of Ithaca Company.

For grenadier Enrico Silva, the other Company set for the southern hemisphere, nor even the other platoons in this one, didn't cross his mind. They hadn't, in a while. Now, all he could focus on were the teeming shadows amid the hedgerows surrounding the clearing.

And how he was on his last belt of ammunition.

4

Sergeant Major Cameron Asano had not believed his eyes during the briefing. How beautiful the surface of

J-726 was, how tranquil and seemingly flawless. The data about its atmosphere and gravity had been the icing on the cake. In the days that followed, aboard the Fleet Corsair set for the dwarf planet, Fourth Platoon's nickname for their destination made sense.

Jade. How fitting.

Since his company first made touch-down, immediate reports weren't comforting. The VTOL he and Fourth Platoon were in, had been redirected.

The order came from above, both literally and in rank. A Brigadier General aboard the sub-orbital Corsair surveying their maneuvers from the comforts of space. Of course, Ithaca Company had the advantage of learning from Gamma's mistakes, or, in Asano's mind, their traumas. At absolutely no fault of their own.

So, the Sergeant Major didn't contest the pilot's compliance of orders. He rerouted the VTOL to assist Third Platoon, half a klick west. Asanao had comforted his men, while simultaneously invigorating them.

After reaching their LZ, which was a mass grave in the making, clearly the enemy's numbers alone had proven more disconcerting than any adjustment in strategy. Each platoon in Ithaca were given two more grenadiers and one more medic than Gamma had been allowed; it wasn't much on paper, but in an ITF combat scenario it played out for the better.

Additionally, grenadiers were permitted two HE hand grenades, against the behest of the Brigadier General's aides.

Assisting one of six platoons that deployed for Jade's southern hemisphere, two hours from nightfall, Asano led a throng of exhilarated infantrymen. Despite their advantages over those that set forth before them, Asano's men were quickly demoralized by the aftermath they witnessed.

There was only some cleaning-up to do, as the platoon they were reinforcing had found their second—or third, or fourth by the looks of it—wind, by the time Asano and company landed.

Wounded natives were still a hassle, apparently, fighting to their final breaths. No matter the limbs they were missing, or the organs.

Although at the other end of the field that Fourth Platoon had disseminated into, Asano would later hear of what some of his men had seen. The soldier closest to the scene was a particularly green Private Ira Harrison. The rifleman was seen flinching and even yelping, on impulse, when a decapitated native sprang to its feet a mere four meters away. It had been partially buried by a soldier whose body was messily halved at the waist, and thus the native's leathery green hide was slathered in red human blood.

The headless native swung its arms madly, weaponless, until a grenadier peppered it with bullets, putting it down for good.

Harrison wouldn't forget that experience, for damn sure.

Asano couldn't quite fathom.

After he and his platoon finished executing strag-glers, they seemed to have incited fear in a few natives that finally withdrew. They retreated into the jungle at the edge of the huge field, pocked by sporadic shrubs and copses.

Several of the mixed platoons' men were ordered by a Corporal Charlie Whitworth, after consulting with Asano, to "safeguard" the nearest jungle treeline. Apparently, Whitworth was officially Third Platoon's surviving highest rank. Their Master Sergeant had literally had his head pulled free from his body by a disarmed native in a tussle that half his men witnessed.

Asano didn't have to examine the young Whitworth's face and eyes to see that the man would need therapy after today. No matter how experienced in ITF combat some of them were—others having only simulations under their belts—war was war.

Ironically, this was not supposed to be anything like *war*. It had been, according to the Fleet in all their wisdom, a plan for a one-sided slaughter. The native population of J-726 being the slaughter*ed*.

Instead, both sides experienced terrible losses.

After leaving Whitworth to tend to some of his own men, Asano spotted two of his own near the edge of a small copse. The cluster of trees had very little underbrush, and didn't seem like much of a threat for the enemy to hide.

A soldier he recognized as Private Ethan Fischer, under Whitworth's "command," was supine on the ground. The life had long left his green eyes, his twenty-year-old face gawking up at the cloud-stippled sky. Fischer's neck had been cut clean through by a native's machete-like weapon, his body half a foot below where his head rested. The dead native was within arm's reach away, at the edge of a small crater made in the soil, by a hand grenade. The lower half of its body was shredded and charred.

"Poor bastard," one of the other infantrymen said, shaking his head.

"The man's a boy, for fuck's sake," Asano said, nudging the Private. He apologized under his breath and crossed himself before turning away.

A medic in Asano's platoon squatted beside Fischer's head. He attempted to close the young man's eyes, but rigor mortis had other plans. The medic cursed quietly and started to look away, but paused.

"Hey, sir. What's this?"

"I don't know, Dell." Asano shrugged, grimacing as he observed the weapon's coarse cutting edge, which ended in an almost rectangular shape. The lower corner had wedged into a gnarled tree root in the ground. Fischer's blood was all over it. "Looks like a mountain man's machete, only…effective."

The medic, Private Dell Torres, clicked his tongue against his teeth and shook his head. Still squatting, he moved over to the left, and gestured at the root on the other side of the machete.

"Nah. This shit."

Asano's brow furrowed. He moved closer, trying to ignore—respectfully—Fischer's decapitated gaze.

Then his own eyes fixated on what Torres was pointing at. A milky substance that seemed to be oozing from the cut root.

"Well," he said, and looked up toward the sky, as if he could see the Corsair among the stairs. "I'll be damned."

Cauldron Quarry

"Where machine fails, man triumphs. But to think that man could reach that point without machine in the first place, is foolish."

W.S. McCaffrey

1

The twelve-pound steel casing hit the dry earth with a loud clanking sound. None of the pilots present could hear it over the thunderous roar of a 90mm Autocannon firing. One round after the other, two seconds between.

In his cockpit, sound-dampened but not immune to the reverberations of the weapon, Donnie Prescott bit down. His mouthpiece absorbed the pressure as the cockpit rattled and so did everything in his body.

"You should see the other guy," he thought to himself, hoping to pitch that line to someone in a pub. Supposing, of course, that he survived this brawl.

He could just about imagine what the other pilot was experiencing. Likely—amidst a storm of blaring alarms from armor integrity to heat warnings—not very well.

Through his ferroglass canopy, thirty feet off the ground, he witnessed the destruction of his opponent.

Their Mech was gradually disintegrating under the relentless artillery fire. Donnie's 90mm Autocannon, mounted on his *Adder*'s right arm, continued to slingshot round after round; the recoil shook the cockpit and each reload was a loud *clang* that echoed through the war machine.

His opponent piloted a Middleweight, however, so it really didn't stand a chance against Donnie's Heavy. Armor was shorn away in chunks and slivers, the Autocannon volleys not its only attackers.

One of Donnie's two teammates circled the enemy *Brawler* to herd it away from their objective. They couldn't let the Mech reach its original target, a factory operated by their employer. Excalibur Construction paid too damn well for them to have turned down the job, much less fail now.

Its competition, however, had proven more pigheaded than expected. Nothing that the Mud Wolves couldn't handle, as Donnie had already put one of their mercenaries out of commission, two klicks south of here. The *Lancer* could not be salvaged, unfortunately, nor did its pilot survive the explosion of its engine.

Kit Sinclair piloted her own Middleweight around behind the enemy, who pivoted the *Brawler*'s torso to try facing her. And to avoid receiving a fatal blow to the thinner armor on any Mech's backside.

"Thanks, Kit," Donnie said through his mouthpiece, a muffled quip. He aligned his next shot, toggling his weapon groups and giving the Autocannon a rest.

His enemy savored the hiatus of artillery, which gave the pilot a chance to retaliate, too. Donnie's canopy splashed green from a medium-bore Laser, but it didn't come close to cutting through. And it missed any of his anterior armor.

He shook his head, disappointed in the enemy pilot. In the next second, Donnie squeezed the trigger on his joystick and lit up the Middleweight. His own Mech's left-arm PPC stabbed a helical beam of blue lightning, which cracked through the air with a similar sound, into the *Brawler*'s right shoulder joint. The internal actuator exploded, its V-shaped arm dropping to the desert earth by its feet. Sparks and fire spewed from the jagged wound, paired with an azure plume of ion waste from the discharged PPC.

A bonus to hitting any Mech with a particle projector cannon was the brief impairment of their electronic systems. The sheer impact alone forced the *Brawler* to teeter, but not fall. Then it stopped moving altogether.

"You think this bastard's bat-shit enough to immolate?" Kit asked, over their private channel.

"Possibly. You'd have to have a few nuts loose to begin with, coming at a powerhouse like Excalibur."

"True. Permission to cripple?" Kit's *Shieldmaiden* had a PPC integrated into its right arm. She lowered her aim, targeting the *Brawler*'s legs.

Toppling a Mech triggered fail-safes that couldn't be overridden, and would immediately shut its fusion engine down to prevent core instability.

Some pilots, those who had a death-wish and the desire to damage nearby enemies in the process, could scuttle their Mech. Given the explosive consequence of this maneuver, pilots called it "immolating." This required manually disengaging containment coils in a painstaking process only used for engine maintenance in a controlled environment. If a pilot was daring, or experienced enough, they could trigger a meltdown and eject in the same maneuver, but there was no guarantee they'd clear the blast.

Anything within a sixty-meter radius would be vaporized, though the white-hot explosion was more horizontal than vertical.

"If you go to cripple, he might have more incentive to immolate," Donnie said, already backpedaling.

"Makes me wanna put some space between us, *then* execute the lunatic."

"It's only a theory, Kit, for fuck's sake," Donnie said, trying not to smirk. He shook his head. "At any rate, that's a negative. Excalibur insists on salvage rights."

"Oh, yeah. The bonus." Kit began backpedaling her *Shieldmaiden*.

Suddenly the *Brawler* went into a crouch, its hocked legs providing this capability. Humanoid Mechs couldn't crouch, though the maneuver was rarely used in combat. Crouching a Mech at the verge of defeat usually preceded immolation, as a meltdown had a better chance of crippling nearby Mechs, especially those just at the edge of the blast radius.

"Fuck me, he's gonna—" Kit's transmission became a sea of static over their com-link when the *Brawler* was engulfed in a blinding orb of light. The blast extended in a white-hot disc of overheated plasma, paired with a violent gust of pressure.

The *Shieldmaiden* was twenty tons lighter, and thus nimbler, than Donnie's *Adder*, which was nonetheless relatively agile for a Heavyweight. Kit only felt a passing tremor and heat spike in her cockpit, nothing more. Donnie, unfortunately, was jarred enough to lose his helmet and nearly dislocated a shoulder against his harness in the process. The *Adder*'s rotund torso rocked turbulently but its hocked legs maintained balance.

Six seconds after the meltdown, all the light had dissipated and only a few tongues of amber flame licked out of the *Brawler*'s remains. Rubble of its feet, melted into a shallow crater in the dry earth, and a miraculously intact left arm were all that remained. Cockpit and canopy, vaporized.

Kit searched the gray sky for a parachute.

The pilot had not ejected.

She shook her head, more irate than sad. Angry that a machinehead would deliberately perish so irreverently. So needlessly.

Not to mention on such a bleak planet.

UMB-2, one of the only two inhabitable rocks in the Orion system, was named after its umbilical-like function to this side of the galaxy, providing various industrial needs thanks to fruitful mining operations on surrounding planets.

Unsurprisingly, this made the atmosphere harsh and virtually unbreathable without proper equipment. UMB-2 was among the driest, most barren colonies in the galaxy. UMB-1 was tied for this title.

"How you lookin', boss?" Kit eventually asked. She could finally see her leader's *Adder* against the backdrop of an encroaching sunset. Its brown and black paintjob—clan colors for the Mud Wolves—gave it a hint of camouflage on terrain like this, especially under low light.

Kit highlighted the thirty-foot Mech for analysis. Armor integrity was at 87%, which she suspected he had suffered from the gunfight earlier. Barely a scratch, by any means. His heat levels were at a startling 73% but slowly falling.

"You read me, Donnie?" She began to accelerate in her direction, giving the *Brawler* crater a wide berth.

"I got you, Kit. Shaken is all. Lost my can."

"No shit. Anything broken?"

"Negative. Shoulder hurts like a bitch, though."

"Grab a tissue and don't let Wyatt hear you whine about it."

Donnie smirked, shaking his head and looking around his cockpit for his helmet. It had rolled into the far right corner. He craned his neck, which hurt as well, and saw that it appeared to be stuck under a bulkhead bench.

"Where is that caveman, anyway?" Donnie asked, glaring at his helmet as if a best friend who decided to bail on a party.

"Hell if I know. Last I saw, he was chasing a pair of *Cicadas* that slipped past him, toward the factory."

"Shit, it would take a *horde* of *Cicadas* to do that place any damage."

"They could light up an outbuilding or two, but…" Kit rotated her Mech's torso to the right, surveying the direction of the factory. It was a sprawling industrial complex befitting of UMB-2. An aesthetic funeral occupying 152 acres. Six outbuildings, each about thirty by fifty meters, arrayed its outer perimeter. Two were barracks for security personnel, three were lodging quarters for workers, and one was waste management.

The latter was nearest Kit and Donnie, about two-hundred meters away. A squat, two-story building that looked like a large, flat black rectangle against the diminishing light. The factory itself was another eighty meters past that.

"Their main objective is Excalibur's hub of operations, not its personnel. That'd just be murder."

"The *Brawler* immolated, Kit. On a sabotage mission, no less. I don't think we're dealing with run-of-the-mill mercs, here."

She sighed. "True."

They both knew that he or she could've very well ejected, had they been dexterous enough. It was also quite possible that their orders prohibited abandoning their Mech. As Donnie insinuated, a fight to the death was rare in the sabotaging business. Of course, Mech pilots' convictions varied just as much as their employers' conditions might.

For the Mud Wolves, though a highly recommended crew, they still had ethics. This didn't save them from being ruthless when they needed to be, however. Most pilots-for-hire loathed the term "mercs," even if they did in fact kill for money. Donnie and his team didn't mind, though—whatever landed them fruitful jobs.

If the other parameters were met.

As Donnie disengaged his harness to retrieve his helmet—not even a veteran could do without it, ideally—Kit whistled. The kind of whistle a man would perform at the sight of a beautiful woman.

Or, in this case, a ninety-ton *Raider* circumventing the far end of the factory. Three-hundred meters out, Kit's systems couldn't provide a readout on Wyatt's Mech, but against the red-orange glow of UMB-2's sunset, she could see a column of smoke trailing its left shoulder. The humanoid war machine could stand toe-to-toe with an *Odin*, at fifty feet tall, but with more firepower and armor. Unfortunately, this also made the *Raider* unnervingly slow, even at full-throttle.

Behind it pursued two *Cicadas*, Lightweight Mechs that resembled tiny *Mastodons*, minus the tusk-like barrels. Waist-high on the *Raider*, they were primarily for scouting and creating diversions, the latter having baited Wyatt forty minutes ago. Thus, taking the imposing Mech out of the equation for the *Brawler* and *Lancer* that Donnie put to rest moments later.

"Well," Donnie sighed. "At least he's taken their interest off of the factory."

"Looks like he's going for a Wolfnet." Kit smirked. She admired Wyatt Palmer's arguable balls-of-steel, though she would never openly admit it, because that would just inflate his already swollen ego. Besides, half the time what seemed like courage was really just Wyatt being a reckless, selfish SOB.

On rarer occasions, he actually put to use his fourteen years of piloting experience.

This seemed like one of them. Kit wanted to believe so, anyway. Donnie had coined the term Wolfnet, though Kit had been the first to improvise it in the field. A simple strategy on paper—drawing an enemy into a calculated crossfire. The maneuver was usually clear-as-day, hard to pull on pilots with any common sense. Clearly, the two *Cicada* operators weren't the sharpest tools in the shed.

"Getting into position," Donnie said, unexcitedly. The last time he assisted Kit in a Wolfnet, unsurprisingly led by Wyatt as well, he took a cluster of missiles to the face.

Kit had blamed the lunar eclipse that was occurring at the moment. Donnie let it slide, but sometimes played it up, his way of flirting. It tickled Kit, but not enough for her to bite.

Not the way he wanted, anyway.

"About time," Kit said, the second Wyatt's *Raider* appeared on her HUD map, as a blue arrow. Its distance measured in "mtrs," a number that began as 100 and gradually decreased.

Their com-link rated to a hundred meters, Kit knew the pilot could hear her. It wasn't unlike Wyatt to play it quiet one minute, and talk your ear off the next. He was a strange creature. As terrifying a pilot as he could be, though, pardons were given.

"You think these assholes are dumb enough to fall for this?" Donnie asked, in position, directly opposite Kit. Fifty meters between them, an unmarked path that Wyatt seemed dead-set on following.

Sixty meters out.

The sunset was to Donnie's back, but Kit had time to make the proper adjustments for her visor, to prevent glare.

"Dumb enough to chase Wyatt's fat ass around Excalibur," she answered.

Donnie smirked. His right hand tightened around the joystick, thumb hovering over a red firing stud. The *Cicadas* both displayed on his targeting system, and appeared virtually undamaged, which meant they must have never gotten out in front of Wyatt.

Smart enough to do that, anyway.

"I heard that, Kit-For-Brains," Wyatt sneered.

She smiled, despite her resentment for that nickname. Wyatt was old enough to be her or Donnie's father, and had that level of humor, even at this point in humanity's future. A sucker for bad puns and wordplay, he couldn't resist it, so Kit gave him a pass.

Until better suited to retort.

Wyatt let off the throttle in the last ten paces, to guarantee that the *Cicadas* were baited. He didn't want them to notice the trap and reroute at the last second. Sure enough, they didn't, at least not until it was too late. He liked to imagine their cockpits bursting with profanity and screams as the other two Mud Wolves ran a gauntlet on them.

Kit's SRMs pelted the *Cicada* nearest her, its left shoulder and that side of its cockpit blossoming flame from six metal-composite armor-piercing warheads. Short-range missiles lacked homing capabilities and were used like explosive buckshot within forty meters. Paired with her two torso-mounted medium-bore Lasers that gouged through melted armor, the *Cicada* pilot was likely drowning in alarms as its armless torso rocked on skinny legs.

Simultaneously, Donnie struck the *Cicada* on the right with both of his PPCs, bringing his heat levels from 0-60% in the blink of an eye. The results were worse for the enemy pilot, their *Cicada* knocked asunder, crashing into the other Lightweight Mech.

The two *Cicadas* fell, a mess of tangled ferrosteel legs and melted armor. Their compact fusion engines shut-down automatically, and the pilots became prisoners within their own machines.

Kit and Wyatt whooped victoriously.

"Another triumphant Wolfnet, I'll be damned," Wyatt eventually added.

Donnie merely smirked wryly and shook his head. He was still dissatisfied with the fate of the *Brawler*, and thus the eradication of Excalibur's bonus.

He turned his *Adder* away from the fallen Light-weights, equally disappointed in their competence as pilots.

"Let Excalibur deal with them," he said into the crew's com-link. "Though I doubt their status as respectable pilots will be salvageable."

Nobody could argue with this.

Donnie led the trio back toward the remains of the enemy *Lancer* that he had inadvertently executed earlier. It would have been a more harrowing battle had Donnie not been assisted by Kit. Thanks to a misjudgment on his part, however, the *Lancer*'s fusion core was breached, and a meltdown devoured the Middleweight. The pilot had managed to eject, but the blast caught him before his parachute could fully deploy.

Their return to the site was to confirm that they had in fact seen the pilot's death. Donnie had a moment of regret and guilt as his *Adder* stood by the craterous remains of the *Lancer*, while his cohorts doubled back.

Wyatt's *Raider* paused twenty meters away, pivoted on its blocky feet, and looked back at Donnie's Mech. Despite its lack of humanoid features, the *Adder* was nonetheless a mechanical extension of its pilot. Great pilots and their Mechs shared this dichotomy, and any respectable machinehead could see it in the smallest motions.

Just as Wyatt could perceive Donnie's pensiveness and gloom by the lingering stance of his *Adder*. The torso, bowed a mere ten degrees, like a head held in shame.

"Unavoidable," Wyatt said into their com-link. His voice grim and empathetic. "Human error. It's inescapable in the heat of battle. Try not to beat yourself up too much over it. You're alive, aren't you?"

Donnie straightened the *Adder* and put its back to the destroyed *Lancer*. To UMB-2's slowly perishing sunset.

"For better or for worse," Donnie said. "Yeah. I sure as hell am."

Wyatt's response had a slight lilt of humor that both Donnie and Kit treasured, whenever it revealed itself.

"Then let's go celebrate, somewhere that isn't this shithole, and you can mope on your own time."

A snorting chuckle punctuated Donnie's return to form, and he proceeded to lead the Mud Wolves toward the factory to collect their reward.

2

Utensils rattled and a few cups fell over when the base of Donnie's fist struck the table. Kit's face fell into her hand, index finger and thumb kneading her temples. She felt his frustration, but was also too familiar with how short-fused he could be. Wyatt merely sighed and paced in the mess hall as their discussion never really left the ground.

Likewise, their ship's landing gear was still on UMB-2. After reviving its stellarator engine from a deep slumber, the crew put their Mechs to rest in its cargo hold. Composing the widest point of the kite-shaped 8200-ton B-class freighter's hull, the cargo hold was fit for two Mechs, but modifications had been made for a third.

Due to this adaptability, Wyatt elected to call their ship the *Chimera*. A designation not yet registered by any other B-class freighter in the galaxy, it stuck.

Unfortunately, the ship was still a slave to their command. Only Wyatt and Kit were licensed pilots for such a craft, often interchanging roles in the cockpit per a rotating schedule. Donnie knew his way around a stellarator transit drive, so he—and occasionally Wyatt as well—served as the *Chimera*'s chief mechanic.

Their reason for remaining on UMB-2 was to no fault of the ship's. The crew's return to the *Chimera* was with grave haste, and an ever greater urgency to leave the planet than before. Donnie had seated himself at the round white table at the far end of the room. Past it was a sealed door leading to the lavatories and living quarters.

It didn't take him long to overheat and pound his fist against the table.

Despite Kit's frustration with his anger, she didn't say anything, and neither did Wyatt, because it was justified.

They had just come from the Excalibur factory. Wyatt had to nearly bar Donnie from attacking their employer when he refused to pay out their full reward. They were aware of the optional bonus for leaving an enemy Mech intact for salvage. They did not, however, realize there was a *penalty* for meltdowns. This incurred a deduction from their total sum, equivalent to one-quarter the original amount.

Donnie wasn't the only one irate, but it wasn't the first time they had been shafted by an employer.

"Materials *and* work are hiking all over the galaxy," Donnie growled through his teeth, one hand now raking through his loose bangs. Dark hair cut short along the sides but left long on the top, previously slicked back, now hung freely from his head like spider-legs.

That he made a good and obvious point increased the frustration in his cohorts, yet only silence followed.

With the increase of repair costs in every known system, it was becoming harder for mercs to operate independent of the Fleet. They weren't qualified for Fleet contracts because of Donnie's history of "violent insubordination" as an infantrymen, eleven years ago. Two years before he linked up with Wyatt, and then ten months before recruiting Kit, too. That was when they christened themselves as the Mud Wolves, and began seeking jobs.

It was easier back then.

Lower costs for repairs and munitions.

Contracts themselves seemed less perilous, too. At least risk-vs-reward wise.

"Donnie, the world is a shit-show," Wyatt finally said, placing his weathered palms flat on the curved table opposite him. His own shoulder-length, bushy brown hair hung forward to frame his face. "And I'm not just talking UMB-2."

With a disgruntled sigh, seeing where Wyatt was going with this and hating that he agreed so simply, Donnie's head lifted slightly. His dark eyes stared back at Wyatt. Waiting for the magic words.

"But can we *please* just leave this dump in the rear-view, and figure it out *up there*—after a decent night's sleep and some grub in the gut?"

The corner of Donnie's mouth curled up, but it would barely validate as a smirk.

"*You're* the pilots," he said with a mustered drone of a voice. "What're we waiting for?"

Wyatt nodded, his lips sucked in. Then he stood up, shrugged, and began to disrobe his Mech jumpsuit en route to the bow of the *Chimera*. He would occasionally walk the ship in as little as his briefs, at the crew's distaste. They didn't feel strongly enough about it to enforce a rule or demand he change his behavior. It had merely become another strange notch in the rope of Wyatt's behavior.

"Kit!" he called from the open doorway at the head of the mess hall. To his left was the scullery, and his right the galley.

Straight ahead, past the threshold, was a narrow path leading to the cockpit.

"You mind?" Wyatt added, raising his bushy eyebrows. On par with his dense beard and long hair, Wyatt was a hairy man. His chest and stomach harbored forests of their own. Visible, now, as the top half of his jumpsuit dangled from his bare waist.

"Copilot duties?" Kit asked, brow furrowed, as she circumvented the table. She gave Donnie's back a pat en route to the front of the ship.

"Duh," Wyatt said, beginning to turn. He paused, and glanced back, shrugging. "Unless you wanna shed your snakeskin, too. Hell, I don't see why you and Donnie don't."

Kit tutted and shook her head.

"In your dreams, pal."

This, at least, made Donnie smirk slightly, though he kept facing forward, his back to them.

"Hey, I'm just saying," Wyatt shrugged. "At least y'all are *fit* to be naked. I'm a sight for sore eyes."

Kit grimaced. "No, you're not."

"No, no. What I'm saying is…I'm a sight that *causes* sore eyes." He scoffed. "Shit, at least I'm self-aware."

Kit smirked, now, too, and shook her head as she reached the open door.

"Right. That you are. And no—pass." She paused with a boot on the threshold, as Wyatt proceeded toward the cockpit. Kit glanced back, just as the *Chimera*'s stellarator engine whirred to a full idle. She raised her voice. "I vote Donnie be a *real* captain and lead by example!"

Kit waited for Donnie to turn, but he only shook his head. She pictured him grinning, and it was enough for her to as well. Then she withdrew, letting the steel door slide shut in her wake.

At the table, Donnie's hand coursed over his face, as if literally wiping the grin off. What replaced it was a sullen expression that was robbed of anger, but not frustration.

To his credit, at least, there was more than a modicum of deliberation that followed. Ill-tempered as Donnie Prescott could be, he was the crew's self-appointed leader for a reason. He had more direction and initiative than either Wyatt or Kit, despite the prior's age and occasional sagacity.

His only dilemma now was making a decision that wouldn't drive them right into fire. Entirely skipping the proverbial frying pan in the process.

***

The freighter seemed at home in the expanse of space. At least its crew felt this way, capable of finding solace within themselves when they gazed out a porthole, versus surveying some planet they had landed on. The environments varied over the years, but most were bleak. There were not a whole lot of colonized planets in their explored galaxy that reminded them of Earth.

A small handful, green and blue from orbit, but devoid of the overpopulation and pollution that tarnished humanity's home. These were seldom visited for work, as they were relatively peaceful. And, for once, mankind managed to keep it this way, but nothing was perfect.

Planets like UMB-1 and 2 were definitely among the dreariest. Grateful for have finally left the place, especially after their bittersweet experience, the Mud Wolves had rerouted to the Ursa system.

There was no agenda, except to rally some repairs and then seek new work. It had already been debated, albeit in passing, whether or not they should plot for Antila next. The crew felt they were in dire need of some R & R, as the Excalibur Construction job had been their second contract in a row without proper respite.

"A man needs some booze and the touch of a woman every now and then to remind himself that life is worth living."

Donnie didn't wholeheartedly agree with Wyatt's ancient advice but neither he nor Kit could argue with the underlying message.

Rest and relaxation was a necessary escapism for people in their line of work. No matter the attached vices, as long as they didn't lose themselves in the cesspool of hedonism, everything solved itself by the time they were wheels-up again.

This had proven true every instance they sought R & R. Whether it was after one job or three consecutive, on Antila where the pubs and entertainment were top-tier for non-family types, or on Canis Three where they could imagine they were on Brosia for a quarter the price.

Life could be good.

If they survived the battles.

"Should we find a job in Ursa, we'll delay R & R 'til after," Donnie had declared, the morning after their return to space. The *Chimera*'s route to the Ursa system was an estimated seven days. "If we *don't*, then maybe we'll answer the calling that we've been ignoring from Canis Three."

Wyatt and Kit couldn't argue.

They toasted to it, stout glasses clinking and Star Mule bourbon swirling in each. The crew proceeded to catch a buzz and seek more quality shut-eye before their journey began again.

Ursa was a home away from home for most machineheads. The origins of the Mechs they piloted, and the continuing hub for production, upgrades, repairs, and munitions. There were other places in the galaxy that offered these necessities, and often at lower prices, but were cheaper quality.

"You get what you pay for" was a timeless adage that never rang truer for Mech pilots.

Three days from reaching Ursa, however, Donnie called for a meeting. Wyatt had been sprucing up the cockpit of his *Raider* while Kit was working out around the feet of her *Shieldmaiden* when Donnie's voice permeated the ship. It was unavoidably tinny on the PA system, but even as bounced off the bulkheads, Wyatt and Kit could discern something else.

Donnie sounded urgent, despite his request entailing the words "at your convenience," a hint of passivity unlike him.

Kit waited for Wyatt to debark from his *Raider*—an unfurled composite rope-ladder helping—before they headed out of the cargo hold. There was no debate between them that Donnie sounded both excited and worried in his call.

They soon found out why.

Kit and Wyatt sat several feet apart on the aft side of the table in the mess hall. Attentive, hands clasped. Donnie stood before them, a boot raised up on the curved seat in front of him. A stance, and the determined look on his face, not easing their qualm—but intensifying their curiosity.

"Before y'all lose your shit, try to let me speak," Donnie began.

Kit and Wyatt's brows furrowed and they looked at each other before shrugging.

"Go for it," Kit told Donnie.

He sighed. "So, I dropped a word on the wire, for a job. But instead of doing what we normally do, I omitted manpower."

A long pause as they stared back at him.

"How'd you specify?" Wyatt asked. "Distance? Something in the system?"

Not Ursa, of course. Despite being the home to mass-produced war machines and munitions, it was a solar system devoid of conflict. And prohibited of executing contracts, though they were often crafted or signed within its boundaries. Fugitives or bounties could flee to Ursa, and while it wasn't heavily policed, the Fleet's cooperative presence with the industry persuaded most convicts and targets to avoid the system altogether.

"Negative," Donnie said. Another pause. "Payout. Upwards of…half a mil."

"Good Lord," Wyatt impulsively said, eyes widening and blinking rapidly as he sat back.

Kit scoffed. "You have a death-wish or something? Or is this just to tickle your curiosity and incur a few wet dreams?"

Donnie half-smirked, shaking his head. Then his expression sobered.

"This is legit." He jabbed a finger on the tabletop. Hard enough to make the decanter of water nearby vibrate. The solemnity in his eyes alone conveyed the gravity of his words. "The job's on Elnath. That's a hop, skip, and a jump away."

"Wonderful," Kit said, throwing her hands up. She let them slap the table on their way down. "Who's your crew?"

Donnie rolled his eyes.

Wyatt, however, was leaning forward again, squinting at him.

"Elnath. That's right over in Taurus. I thought that place was barren."

"It ain't pretty," Donnie said, trying to restrain his excitement, as he detected a sense of intrigue in Wyatt.

Which, for a Mech pilot as daring as him, usually heralded approval. "But, apparently, two years ago it was terraformed. Simple, given the easygoing atmo. Similar to Orion. Elnath isn't far off, either. Turns out it became a prospect for miners, but—"

"But to no avail," Wyatt said, nodding. "Yeah, I remember hearing about that. Nothing of any merit on that rock."

"Until now, it seems," Donnie said, resolve in his voice and eyes. "According to the contract, Starchitect Enterprises has not only set-up shop on Elnath, but struck gold. So to speak. The target site is Cauldron Quarry, seven klicks from the Pollux Crater, which would theoretically be our infil."

"Sabotage," Kit said, plainly and unenthusiastically. "This is a sabotage mission."

"Correct," Donnie said. "*But*, the contract does anticipate heavy opposition. Apparently, they've got an inside man working for Starchitect."

Kit's eyebrows raised. She scooted forward, edge of her seat, elbows supporting her torso and hands clasped together. Donnie tried to hide his relief, in seeing that he had finally sundered Kit's disinterest.

"That's…quite an advantage," Kit admitted. Her brow proceeded to furrow again. "I can't imagine why such an advantage—going into a job—would still render a high pay-out. What's the catch?"

"Starchitect is…heavily armed."

"To guard a…mining facility." Kit's skepticism had taken a full circle.

Donnie sighed. "Let's just say, whatever they found on Elnath is worth defending, tooth and nail."

"More like flesh and bone. What are we talking, here? Two dyads?" She scoffed. Her palms on the table. "A *faction*, for Christ's sake?"

Donnie shrugged. Squinting.

"Is there a name for eight?"

"*Eight* fucking Mechs?" Kit nearly exclaimed. She let out a sardonic laugh. "Donnie, you and Wyatt might have your own wild death-wish, but I'm not gonna go on some suicide run for half a mil."

"Would you go for the full seven digits?"

Kit suddenly looked at him as if he had insulted her entire lineage.

"Don't act like you aren't a daredevil in the cockpit, too, Kit." Donnie stood up and jabbed a finger in her direction. He wasn't going to tiptoe anymore. "If you were a prude of any caliber you wouldn't be here. Fact."

Kit scoffed, shook her head, and crossed her arms. Wyatt sighed beside her, kneading his brow for several second before inviting himself back into the discussion.

"Who made the contract? Excalibur? Valor Mining?"

Donnie stared at Kit for two more seconds, her gaze avoiding his. Then his eyes found Wyatt, settled for a full Mississippi, and finally he answered. His voice monotonous so that every syllable made a solemn impact.

"Ferrocore Industries."

Wyatt's eyes widened for a moment. Kit simply shook her head, though Donnie knew she was still processing this possibility.

"Half a mil, no wonder," Wyatt said.

"Remember," Donnie added. "I said *upwards* of half. More like seven. And you know what else? They're offering *half in advance*, the rest upon confirmation. Wired, on-site. No bullshit."

"Ferrocore is a partner of Ursa Steel, for fuck's sake," Kit said. "They have *Fleet* resources, why would they dump seven-hundred-thousand on mercs just to wipe out a mining compound?"

A few seconds of silence stretched between them, Donnie watched Wyatt compute it in his head. And then Wyatt let his thoughts break the quiet.

"If they do it independently, they can ensure owner's rights, which makes any bartering with the Fleet all the more lucrative."

Kit realized what he said was true, and everything else lined up. Paired with the half-now half-later deal, a rare parameter for sabotage jobs, not to mention the unprecedented sum, she couldn't ignore the temptation.

"I just don't…" Kit began to say, but stopped, and kneaded her temples with both hands.

Wyatt leaned forward. "How many bites has the contract gotten? And what's Ferrocore's window?"

"Window is twelve days. Just shy of two weeks—enough time for us to repair, resupply, and reroute to Taurus."

Kit straightened, as if a light bulb just went off above her head. Only, it didn't seem like the good kind.

"Wait, wait." She then smirked, her expression suggesting that this was some kind of bad joke. "Three-v-eight? Real funny, Donnie. Too twisted, even for you two."

Wyatt sighed. "She's right, boss. I hate to break it to you, but we're no faction. There's reckless, and then there's suicide. I suspect the eight Mechs they have on-site aren't *Cicadas*, either."

"Three Heavies, three Mediums, one Light, and a pair of *Tarantulas*. According to the contract."

"Goddamn," Kit muttered.

Wyatt whistled. "Yeah, bud. I don't know what's going on in that crazy head of yours, but we're one more than a dyad, and one short of a squad. Two Heavies, and one Medium."

"Kit pushes that *Shieldmaiden* like a Heavy on Lightweight legs."

A fair observation, given its Middleweight class, but Kit accepted the compliment on her behalf, too.

"I appreciate the vote of confidence," she said, "but don't be stupid. This kind of intel makes it a numbers game, simple as that. So, we're two shy of a faction, but let's be honest, the best ones are six or seven strong."

Donnie backed away from the table, turned one step, and paused. A smirk graced his handsome face, and two loose scythes of hair hung across his left eye. His unwavering confidence in this job had begun as an irritation to Kit, but now it was starting to turn on her. Like an infection settling into her bloodstream, whether she liked it or not.

"Ye of little faith," Donnie finally said. He faced them again, several feet away from his side of the table. "Who's to say we can't *become* a faction? Just for Cauldron Quarry, anyway."

They stared at him quizzically.

"Two words, two pilots," Donnie said, bluntly but with a wisp of arrogance. A pause followed, one he allowed for dramatic effect. "Wanted by the Fleet for going AWOL, claiming that riches surpass duty. If that's not a sign of who to employ, then I don't know what is."

"*We* don't employ," Kit practically snapped. "We *get* employed. Besides, who the living hell are you even talking about?"

Donnie half-turned away from them again. This time seemingly more resolute about walking away. Once more he stalled, glanced back toward them, and smirked—almost deviously.

"The best twins this side of the galaxy, to ever pilot seventy tons of ferrosteel."

Kit shook her head, expression slackening.

"No. No fuckin' way."

Donnie shrugged. "If you want off, you'll have a chance to on Ursa, when we get repairs and resupply. Sorry, Kit—there were three bites on the contract when I signed it. I don't bite, I eat; and we all gotta eat."

"You *took* the contract!?" Kit exclaimed.

Wyatt couldn't help but smile to himself, in awe of Donnie's cold initiative. In a way, irreverent of their opinions, but it was clear that he was dead-set on taking the job regardless of their company.

There was something admirable about it, to Wyatt anyway. He hoped that in the coming days, Kit would see it this way as well.

"Let it cook, Kit," Donnie said, on his way out of the mess hall. "We're a few days from Ursa, but should be able to link up with the others in Taurus, and make good time on the contract."

"Have you even *spoken* to the Twins yet?"

"I buzzed them. They're not off-planet 'til tomorrow. Just finished a job on Alzirr. That's all I know right now."

"No shit," Wyatt said, feeling a stir of confidence. "Alzirr's in the Ptolemy system. That's like, within arm's reach of Taurus."

A plain exaggeration, of course.

"One could say…it was meant to be." Donnie shrugged. The door before him zipped open. He made fleeting eye contact with Kit. "Five-v-eight is manageable, especially for the Mud Wolves. I mean…name a better dyad than *the* Twin Dragons."

The seven-planet Ursa system embraced them as if distant lovers. Specifically the dwarf planet Alcor, home to some of the best Mech technicians in the galaxy. Each of these specialists, some even a quarter Wyatt's age, were more adept with a Mech's parts than all of the pilots combined.

These men and women were paid well.

By their employer, Ursa Steel, and the occasional tip from generous pilots.

Entrusting their Mechs—armored, complex extensions of themselves—to strangers took a lot of respect for the industry. Some pilots refused to leave a hangar while their machine was worked on; some insisted on occupying the exact bay, not trusting the techs themselves.

This wasn't the case for the Mud Wolves.

Although Kit was still tentative about Cauldron Quarry, much less enlisting the help of the Twin Dragons, she had not voiced her disapproval again since that day. Wyatt's silent consent annoyed her at first, but was motivation to play it quiet, too.

While their Mechs were worked on—limited repairs needed after their last scuffle on UMB-2—Donnie and Wyatt hit a pub five kilometers west of the hangar. The Saddern was a favorite pit-stop for pilots on Alcor. Teeming with machineheads from all walks of life, quarrels were common but the booze was worth it. The prices, especially. Another four kilometers southeast and they could enjoy a finer establishment with even finer spirits—the Magnetar. As expected, though, at nearly triple the cost.

They passed.

Today, anyway.

"After Cauldron Quarry, we might exclusively buy Magnetar," Wyatt jested, already three bourbons deep.

"Shit, after Cauldron, we'll set up our own little Magnetar on the *Chimera*." Donnie had built his own sufficient buzz thanks to two Supernova shots. The clear film of vodka made his lips glisten. "You'll never have to hear the empty clinking of Star Mules ever again."

Wyatt was ready to toast another glass to that fantasy, when a passing brute of a man bumped into the back of his stool. Wyatt wobbled briefly and began to exchange blubbering words with the other drunken pilot. Donnie's intoxicated attempt to quell their beef was futile at best, but nullified when Kit strode into view.

It was more of a sauntering, embittered march than a model's strut. But to the Saddern's patrons, who were three-quarters male, it was the sexiest sight this side of Ursa.

She had come from a smaller joint two blocks down, called the Ishtar. Named after the Mesopotamian goddess of fertility and war, the tavern was a hub for female pilots only, and offered a comfortable quality between the Saddern and Magnetar.

Women, even pilots of great fortitude, seldom chanced attending the Saddern. Presently, Kit's guest appearance made the teetering fight come to a stand-still, just long enough for Donnie to drag Wyatt out. Kit tipped the bartender with an extra coin and gave a taunting wink to the brute who would have sent Wyatt into the neighboring system.

She managed to slip out of the pub without getting accosted, and joined her cohorts on the street.

"You can thank me when you're sober, I won't count it now," Kit said, striding past them.

They carefully crossed the street at half daylight, Donnie and Wyatt dragging their feet like inebriated yetis. But when Donnie saw Kit trip up a curb, he smirked to himself and elbowed Wyatt. Then he called out to her, as even still she had a ten-second lead on them.

"Likewise!"

"What have I got you to thank for?" Kit asked, now failing to hide her own stupor.

"In a week's time you'll have seven-hundred-thousand things to thank me for!"

Kit slowed down, enough to gather a fraction of her own wits *and* let them catch up. Somewhat.

"Actually, screwball, it'll be more like..." Her eyes danced around for a moment. A few kilometers above them, the thunderous hum of a freighter entered Alcor airspace. It was a common sound on five of the seven Ursa planets, night and day.

"One-forty," Wyatt butted in, surprising them both despite his drunkenness. "But…to be fair, that's like…what we normally split for any other job."

He had a good point.

Their last sabotage contract paid two-hundred thousand, which was on the high-end for that sort of run. Split three ways, not including what they allotted for repairs and resupply, that was only sixty-six thousand each.

"It'd be more if we went alone," Donnie said.

"That's the booze talking," Kit said, trying not to slur her words. "Crazy as you can be, that's not even worth joking about.

On the spot, Donnie would've disagreed. But as time passed and they returned to the *Chimera* to retire for the evening—free room and board compared to paying for an inn—he had to side with her. Merely thinking about tackling this job with only three Mechs, no matter how competent their pilots, was anxiety-inducing. Three versus seven made his fingers tingle, and not in the good way.

The *Chimera* was parked in a sheltered lot for freighters while their Mechs were being worked on. Most of the ships in the lot would be here for several days, some as long as a week. The Mud Wolves' machines required minimal attention, and had been given a satisfactory ETA from the techs.

Tomorrow morning, noon at the latest.

At eight, Kit and Wyatt were up. How Wyatt managed a hangover better than Donnie, neither he nor

Kit would ever understand. But by ten Donnie was awake, and ten minutes shy of eleven he was feeling fresher than most might.

Not long after eleven, their techs rang them as a group. Like clockwork, they moved in tandem. The hangar was only a five-minute Mech walk from the ship lot, ample time to deduce if additional repairs were needed. It was also a gesture of good faith from the tech crews themselves, like a guarantee that they had not sabotaged the machines.

Their return to space was made in haste once the three Mechs had boarded the *Chimera* again. Alcor was a gray sphere from orbit, white-mottled by clouds. Wyatt plotted for Taurus, but before engaging the stellarator drive, requested Donnie's presence in the cockpit.

"You rang?" Donnie lumbered into the spacious cabin. He reached the cockpit behind an arching canopy, and peered down.

Kit looked up from the copilot's seat to his right. He wasn't expecting to see her there. Much less with her harness on, long brown hair tied back into a ponytail, eyes glowing with a certain resolve. Always befitting of her.

"Any word from the twins?" Wyatt asked, behind the *Chimera*'s yokes.

"Uh, yeah, actually." Donnie cleared his throat. He looked down at Kit, and brushed his bangs back. "Made up your mind, yet, Ms. Sinclair?"

Her brow furrowed.

"Mrs., right, sorry." Donnie smirked. "You're married to the *Shieldmaiden*. My mistake."

"And yes, I made up my mind before we were wheels-down."

Donnie's eyebrows raised. "That so?"

"You think I'd risk stepping into the Saddern if I wasn't down for one last rodeo?"

Donnie saw a tiny smile grace the microcosm that was Kit's ruggedly beautiful face. He cherished it.

"One last rodeo" was what the Mud Wolves called every job they went on. Because that's what it had the potential of being—their last ride. No matter how much the odds favored them, or how minimal the risks. Anything could go.

"Will you take my gratitude now?" Wyatt asked. "Been sober for three hours."

"Shit, Wyatt, I'd put ten coin down on you *never* being sober." Kit grinned, and Wyatt let out a laugh.

"Fair point. But I appreciate it nonetheless."

"Let's just get this bird going before I change my mind." Kit looked up at Donnie again. "So what did the Dragons say?"

"They'll meet us in-orbit."

Kit's grin faded, but only in exchange for surprise.

"They bit that hard?"

"Their reputation doesn't disappoint," Wyatt said, looking down at his controls and running a routine systems check. Currently, the *Chimera* idled in Alcor's exosphere, occupying a cleared route for departing freighters. In five minutes, that would expire, and the Fleet patrols policing the channels of space between planets would be all over them.

This rarely happened.

"High money, and as they see it," Donnie elaborated, "good odds."

"Five-v-eight," Kit said, blandly.

"*Tarantulas* are all about mobility, not firepower. Nessa alone thinks she can handle them."

Kit shrugged. "I appreciate a cocky gal. Even if it's a bit arrogant to tackle two spiders by herself."

"Nobody will be alone down there," Donnie assured her. "We've put a whole squad on their back, just you and I. These odds favor us. Fuck the numbers."

Kit tried to smirk, but ultimately nodded, shrugging again.

"Might wanna buckle up, boss." Kit flipped a switch on the dash, and the *Chimera*'s transit drive hummed to life. "I wanna make good time."

4

Roy and Nessa Alcott, born in the Draco system thirty-five years ago, had been raised by their father. Their mother perished during childbirth, which must have had a wounding effect on her husband's psyche at the time, because he raised them without much nurturing.

This was the story, anyway.

The Twin Dragons were known by moniker and reputation across the galaxy, by any self-respecting pilot. And most Fleet officials. Though far from pirates or immoral mercenaries, they often overlooked certain tenets if the reward was high enough.

None of the Mud Wolves ever thought they would work with the siblings themselves, directly, though a happenstance bumping-into on Ursa was more than expected. It simply had not occurred.

Meeting them on the umbilical airlock bridge between the *Chimera* and their own C-class freighter was almost uncanny. For Donnie, anyway. He perceived the pilots with reverence, whereas Wyatt held only curiosity, and Kit was far more dubious. She tried to keep this doubt at bay, though, at least on the surface. Exhibiting any sign of disrespect toward pilots she had to work with toward a common goal on a plane of life-and-death was simply bad juju.

"You should see the look on your face, bruv," Roy said, smirking under a black eyepatch as he shook Donnie's hand. A momentarily unyielding grip.

"Yeah?" Donnie asked, trying not to laugh.

"Like a schoolboy meeting his hero," Nessa said, brow furrowing but not able to restrain her own smile.

"Sorry, I've just heard so much," Donnie said. He withdrew his hand, and shrugged. "Frankly, it's about as intimidating to finally work with *the* Twin Dragons, as it is an honor."

"We appreciate that, yeah?" Roy's statement was half a declaration and half a question. He pivoted to nod at his sister, who shared his dark complexion and strong stance. They were both beautiful in their own rights, Nessa leaner in the face and, naturally, figure. But not immensely. The vest she wore over a tank exposed arms that were not devoid of muscle, though her feminine qualities were undeniable, even with a black beret covering her hair.

"Sure, I suppose," Nessa finally said. "As long as you don't get too giddy when it matters most, pretty boy."

Donnie's elated expression faded and he raised his palms.

"Hey, now. I recognize the gravity of this partnership."

"Good, good."

Roy gently elbowed his sister.

"Nice to meet y'all," Wyatt said, stepping forward. "I trust Donnie here has introduced himself, and us, in light of our...*absence*...during his contact with you?"

"Yeah, he has, more or less," Roy said, nodding.

"Well, hell, I'm Wyatt Palmer," he said nonetheless, stepping forward again and offering his hand. The previously austere façade melted away in lieu of a jollier demeanor. Kit almost rolled her eyes, at his flank.

"Right, right, ya know, it's not like we haven't heard of you all, too," Roy said. After their hands parted, he pointed at Wyatt. "You pilot a *Raider*, that right?"

"Yes, sir. Just got her patched up after a run-in with a few naughty *Cicadas*."

Roy smirked, clapping his hands. As his expression dissolved, he squinted at Wyatt.

"Not too bad, I hope."

"Oh, nah, they got their just desserts and my gal is ready for a nastier fight."

Roy nodded. "Glad to hear it."

"And the *Shieldmaiden*," Nessa said, standing obliquely from Kit. She nodded at her. "Yours, I imagine?"

"Yes, ma'am," Kit said. She finally stepped forward, and offered her own hand.

Nessa eyed her head to toe, and seemed briefly disgruntled with Kit's attire. The cargo slacks were typical of a machinehead, unisex, but the snug white tank over a bra was not. Especially in the company of men. It was hardly white, though, sullied by grease and soot. Kit's frame, though lean at a glance, was visibly, strong, too.

A few seconds passed before Nessa smirked, infinitesimally, to herself. Kit and even Donnie saw this as Nessa's realization that Ms. Sinclair could handle herself and looks weren't everything.

"They don't give you any shit for it, do they?" Nessa asked, at last accepting Kit's idle hand, and returning the gesture.

"For what?" Kit raised an eyebrow.

"A woman, piloting a *Shieldmaiden*." Nessa shrugged. "A lot of men would argue that a female has no right to anything but a *Shieldmaiden*."

"You make it sound like an inferior model."

"Not at all. Hell, I've seen an *Odin* be put-down by a *Falcon*, 'cause their pilot was shit-for-brains."

"I bet," Kit nodded, letting a smirk escape her. She shrugged. "Helming a Mech is different than holding a gun."

"Got that right."

"So what's this from?" Donnie asked, pointing at his own eye, facing Roy. "I figured I'd have heard about the one-eyed Roy Alcott."

Roy grinned, and flipped the eyepatch up, impulsively making Donnie flinch. He didn't want to stare into a hollowed, necrotic eye socket without warning. Fortunately, he didn't. Roy's umber iris stared back at Donnie, his eye in perfect health.

Nessa shook her head.

"I'll be damned," Wyatt said, laughing curtly.

"You had me," Donnie said. "So, what's that for? Let me guess. Intimidating rookies?"

"Or bad broads at pubs," Wyatt added. "Those dumb enough to fall for it, anyway."

Kit looked over at him with a furrowed brow. He didn't even notice. He and Donnie were too busy bantering with Roy.

"Shit," he replied, smirking, "can't a man be greedy and say *both*?"

Nessa rolled her eyes, but the three men shared a moment of masculine, albeit goofy camaraderie.

"He's rowdier than I imagined, frankly," Kit muttered, only within Nessa's earshot.

"He thinks highly of the Mud Wolves," Nessa replied, quietly. She could see the surprise on Kit's face. "But, much like his sister, he knows when to nut-up and shut-up."

The corner of Kit's mouth curled up slightly.

"Good to hear. 'Cause this contract won't be a walk in the park."

Nessa nodded. She agreed with Kit, but didn't want to speak on it. Too much acknowledgment of the risks they faced could substantiate it into discouragement. The last thing they needed.

"Hell, I can respect that," Wyatt said, his voice gruff but still full of mirth, as he and Donnie basked in their amusement with Roy. "Afterall, chicks dig scars."

"Pain heals," Roy added, with grim nonchalance.

Wyatt shrugged. "Glory lasts forever."

The men exchanged nods and grins. Donnie took a few steps behind Wyatt to reach Kit.

"See? Look at that. A natural bond. Can't turn a blind eye to that, now can we, Kit?"

"I heard that," Roy snapped, and the men proceeded to laugh some more.

Nessa and Kit rolled their eyes in tandem. A unified groan of strained steel against the steady vacuum of space caught everyone's attention. The airlock sustained, green lights at either end of the sixty-foot umbilical bridge still illuminated.

"Best we cut the chit-chat and get to work, eh?" Nessa told Roy, slapping his shoulder.

"You got the coordinates?" Donnie asked, already backpedaling with his crew.

"Pollux Crater," Roy responded. "Will send confirmation once undocked."

"Copy. Elnath's thirteen hours away." Donnie shouted from the *Chimera*'s end of the umbilical. "Sleep tight!"

"See you planetside!" Nessa added.

They cycled their respective airlocks and reentered each ship.

5

After six hours of Mech prep and systems checks, the two crews were ready for combat. Their machines were, anyway. They proceeded to catch some shuteye, as a long and arduous day awaited them. The aptly named *Wyvern* that Roy and Nessa operated was about twenty tons lighter than the *Chimera*, making it a touch easier to navigate.

As such, it reached Elnath sooner.

Ahead by two hours, but sooner nonetheless.

Since the first half of Ferrocore's contractual payment was wired to the Mud Wolves, and divvied with the Twin Dragons, everyone's level of enthusiasm had inched higher.

With their coordinates synchronized, the crews eventually achieved touch-down in the same LZ, a vast natural crater designated Pollux. Wyatt set the *Chimera* down a safe eighty meters from the *Wyvern,* with still plenty of space on either side of them. By the time the *Chimera*'s landing gear had deployed, both Roy and Nessa had already stretched their mechanical legs. The two war machines patrolled the immediate area ahead of Pollux. Though deemed safe from orbit, additional vigilance couldn't hurt.

Elnath was a predominantly barren, rocky, dry rock of a planet.

According to the intel provided by Ferrocore's contract, Starchitect Enterprises had established a quarry in a manmade crater seven kilometers northeast of Pollux. The pilots' southwest approach of their LZ allowed them to infil undetected. They had the element of surprise, and would relish that for as long as possible.

"Linking your comms," Nessa's distinct voice entered the Mud Wolves' ears, as their Mechs' feet reached the arid terrain outside the *Chimera.*

Its loading ramp slowly shut in their wake, a light gust of dirt passing between them. Inside his *Raider*'s cockpit Wyatt kissed his fist before waving a farewell to the freighter.

"We read you," Donnie said, buckling his helmet. He watched the holographic HUD flicker to life on his visor, and expand onto the *Adder*'s canopy.

It was late morning on Elnath, which offered a twenty-hour day.

As of two years ago, thanks to independent terraforming—a job usually performed by the Fleet—it also provided Earthlike gravity and breathable atmosphere. Still, the planet lacked visible flora or fauna, and was akin the vast deserts back home. Beyond the Pollux Crater extended a seemingly endless ochre plain.

There were so few dunes and ridges in this region that it made the planet appear flat from the pilots' perspectives. Heat refraction, given the 122°F surface temperature, limited their visibility beyond four-hundred meters. Even through polarized ferroglass, and enhanced optics.

"I bet we'll confuse the enemy, the way we look," Wyatt said, referring to their coloration.

The Mud Wolves were distinctly brown with splashes of black, whereas the Twin Dragons were a jungle green with hints of yellow.

"We'll just tally that as one more advantage we won't squander," Nessa said.

"I hear that," Roy chimed.

"Say, Nessa," Wyatt said, observing her *Lancer* through his canopy. "Without tagging you, correct me if I'm mistaken, but are you running twin LBX's on that thing?"

"You sound disappointed."

"On the contrary. Impressive. Most *Lancers* sport ACs. A reason to fear them from afar."

Wyatt's experience spoke volumes in so few words, and it dawned on the other Mud Wolves what he meant. Nessa's *Lancer* was a robust Mech with two massive forward-facing cannons as arms, protruding directly from the shoulders. Pilots typically ran 60-90mm Autocannons from them, or in rarer cases Gauss rifles. The LBX was least common, especially from such long barrels. Though technically an AC variant, the LBX was like a tank-sized shotgun, spraying 20mm cluster munitions that fragmented in flight, peppering the target with small explosions.

As Wyatt had insinuated, most pilots saw a *Lancer* and immediately tried to get closer, as they feared being sniped by its long-range cannons. In Nessa's case, this would work beautifully, as the LBX was most effective within forty meters.

"I get it," Nessa said, her smirk invisible to the others, but a smidgen of it escaped in her voice. "I'm smarter than I look."

"Likewise," Wyatt added, and it seemed the makeshift faction was off to a good start. Communications wise, at least.

The five Mechs assembled two-hundred meters from the crater, with no clear formation or lead. Donnie strode his avian-legged *Adder* toward the front of the group, but Roy had something to say about that, albeit tacitly. His *Kodiak* traipsed ahead of Donnie, the torso twisting to face him as its legs advanced in another direction. Virtually a tuskless *Mastodon* with L-shaped arms, the *Kodiak* had one of the most distinct and imposing silhouettes of any Mech to date. Named after the old great Kodiak bears back home, the design became a signature of reliability for Ursa Steel.

Its torso and horizontal half-egg cockpit turned to the right, facing Donnie as it advanced. Though he couldn't see Roy inside, Donnie pictured him shrugging comically.

Point in fact, Roy Alcott was doing just that. But he didn't keep everyone in silence.

"Sorry, Mud Wolf, but my TAC beats yours."

Donnie couldn't help but smirk and shake his head.

"You have a point," he admitted.

They didn't need to discuss it beyond that. Among them, the *Kodiak* had the most firepower and long-range capabilities, making it an ideal vanguard. The massive, square, twenty-capacity shoulder-mounted missile racks offered a lock-on as far out as 610 meters. Apart from a few larger Mechs, the seventy-ton *Kodiak*'s TAC systems were unmatched. The targeting acquisition module would highlight an enemy Mech and relay its information with a clarity that most machines could gather no farther than three- to four-hundred meters away.

Wyatt's *Raider* sported its own LRMs, too. Canted trapezoidal shoulder-mounted racks guarded from the outside by epaulettes. These vertical armor plates shielded the raised racks from lateral attacks, though like any weapon on a Mech, they were still susceptible to anterior damage.

Unlike the *Kodiak*, though, the *Raider*'s TAC range maxed at five-hundred meters.

There was no debating Roy's assumption of pointman, though the Mud Wolves wouldn't doubt that his sister had the impulse to. Ultimately the makeshift faction found themselves following Roy's *Kodiak* as it spearheaded their formation. Behind him, the pilots fanned out to provide clear lanes-of-fire, safely spaced apart to cover an eighty-meter expanse of the desert.

They walked in lumbering steel strides, at a steady 23kph, for the first two klicks. Approaching the third, Roy suggested they pick up the pace.

"At this rate we'll reach the quarry just under half an hour," he said.

"Action-starved?" Wyatt asked. He shrugged, as if they could see him. "I mean, it's good time."

"Sooner the better. We don't want to hit them when the workers are on a lunch break."

"Wouldn't that be…the ideal time to strike?" Kit thought out loud.

"Not necessarily," Nessa said. "We've hit quarries before, though never ones with this level of security. Still, when the workers are doing their thing, the defense perimeter slackens. Less eyes on them, more room for idleness."

"On break, though," Wyatt chipped in, realizing the merit in their strategy. "The workers, the quarry itself, is more exposed. No activity equals weakness. Security tightens."

"Huh. Makes sense." Kit nodded.

"So…wanna push it to thirty, Roy?" Donnie asked.

"Was thinking more like forty."

"I'm game," Donnie replied, nonchalantly. His left hand gripped the accelerator and prepared to slowly push it forward.

"Hey, sis," Roy followed. "Wanna play tomato?"

Nessa sighed, tangibly, over their com-link.

Wyatt noticed her *Lancer*'s torso swing in his direction, as they continued to stride forward. He pivoted his to the left in acknowledgement. They were nearly fifty meters apart, behind Roy. Behind them, sharing an even bigger gap, were Kit and Donnie.

"Wyatt will join," Nessa said, a sense of surrender on her face. Even relief, though she'd never wholeheartedly admit it. "I hate playing tomato alone."

"What happened to being a strong, independent woman?" Roy asked, his grin almost audible.

"Fuck off," she said, with a click of her tongue.

The lot of pilots smirked to themselves and shook their heads, Kit included.

"Care to fill me in on whatever the hell *playing tomato* is?" Wyatt asked.

Donnie and Kit were glad they didn't have to ask, and pretended, in silence, to know what the Twin Dragons were talking about.

"Well, old man, you and I happen to be the biggest slowpokes of the group." Nessa paused. "Or am I crazy?"

"You might still be crazy, *young lady*," Wyatt replied, smirking through the sarcasm, even though nobody could see his face. His tone was evident, but the intrigue remained. "But you aren't wrong. We max out just under forty."

"Then," she sighed. "We fall back, play the straggler for a few klicks, and *catch up* when needed."

A long pause between them.

"Catch-up. *Ketchup*." Wyatt tutted. "I'm ashamed I didn't get that sooner."

"Roy and I are ashamed for you, old-timer." There was a brief chuckle from Nessa's comms. A seemingly rare moment of humor and humanity from her. "But we suspect you're a quick learner."

"You'd be surprised just how quick," Wyatt said, with a lick of confidence that undeniably sounded like flirting.

"Easy," Roy said, his own lightheartedness carrying over their frequency.

The demeanor of the lot softened in that moment, and some of their reactions could be quietly heard. Wyatt among them, although he didn't defend himself.

What followed was business.

"Accelerating to forty-two," Roy said. His *Kodiak* gradually reached 42mph, its speed indicated on the HUDs of the other pilots. Donnie soon matched his speed, but maintained his right flank. He pivoted his torso as a waving gesture when he passed Wyatt on the right.

Meanwhile, crossing behind Nessa's *Lancer* to throttle ahead of her, was Kit's *Shieldmaiden*.

"I see you back there, Sinclair," Roy said. "I know you could easily leave us all in the dust, try to resist the urge."

"Urge resisted, *Alcott*. Call me Kit, would you?"

"Shit, I just…almost doesn't feel right. Have known y'all for hardly a day."

"My favorite color is green, I prefer Wagner over Bach, and Onyx Exo is my favorite label."

Kit rattled off the info with a wry sense of humor, proving that her statements were true to heart but almost inconsequential.

"No shit," Roy said, sounding genuinely piqued. Then he cleared his throat. "Well, then. *Kit*, is it? Maybe after all this, I buy you a shot or two of Exo and we—"

Kit interrupted him, before Donnie could even think about it.

"If we're drinking Exo, might wanna get your own bottle."

"Goddamn, little brother," Nessa chuckled. "Careful with this one."

Inside her compact cockpit, Kit smiled and shook her head. She now matched Roy's speed, on his left flank.

"Will do," Roy muttered in response.

About ten seconds later, while the three of them advanced ahead of Nessa and Wyatt, the silence on their channel sputtered.

"Uhhh, I thought you were older, Roy?" Donnie asked, his voice low.

"I am, by a *wise* six years," Roy said. "She just calls me that to pull my chain."

Donnie laughed quietly. "Classic siblings."

"You have any?"

"Not by blood," Donnie said, and a moment of pensiveness sapped the joy from his face. "Until it was on my face."

A stall in the forming camaraderie over their com-link. Roy nodded and made the deduction, swifter than anyone else expected, and before Donnie could volunteer an explanation.

"Infantry?" Roy asked.

A tic made Donnie's left eye and cheek flinch. Then he sniffled and lifted his chin, catching a dichotomous view of the desert before him, through both his visor and the canopy. Almost like a broken mirror.

"Yeah, for all of ten months."

"Didn't bode well?" Nessa asked. A pause, her own voice hoarse with empathy. "Seeing your brothers die in your arms...for the Fleet, no less."

"That and…a building, uh, *disagreement* with my superiors." Donnie bared his teeth briefly, then licked them behind his lips, and tried to sober himself up.

"I hear that," Roy said, his voice colliding with his sister's, as they spoke nearly in unison.

"Say," Wyatt said, after another expanse of silence between them. "How are we on time, Roy? And range. My targeting system just flickered a red triangle; gone, the next second."

"Huh. Let's see. Cycling mine, standby."

Roy's last word didn't refer to their progress. The Mechs continued across the ochre plain, each step leaving a three-toed depression in the dry crust. The coloration was beginning to lighten to an almost whitish-brown, and glimpses of arid vegetation intermittently peered through cracks.

"Mine's misbehaving, too," Roy finally said. "Long-range systems are fuzzy. Must be a jammer nearby."

"*How* near, you think?" Kit asked.

"Within a klick, easy."

"High alert," Donnie announced. He uncapped the safety covers from his firing studs.

"LiDAR shows a significant depression one klick north," Roy said. "Confirm?"

"Confirmed," Donnie said.

Then Nessa and Wyatt chimed in, though Kit stayed quiet. Her Middleweight, even though ahead of the other two, had a significantly weaker LiDAR.

"Must be the quarry," Roy said. "I'd say we've made great time, then. Hey—see that? Ridge ahead, two-, three-hundred meters. Slow down."

"Decelerating," Kit said.

Donnie complied, and as it turned out there would be no playing "tomato" for Nessa and Wyatt. They naturally assembled when the others slowed down, as the ridge neared. It stretched across the plain for at least half a kilometer in either direction, and although not abruptly steep, had gradually elevated enough to obstruct their view ahead.

Until they crossed it.

The Mechs came to a complete, contemplative stop once fifty meters from the horizontal peak.

"Fun rock, this one," Kit said, and nobody could argue the sarcasm. The planet was hot, dry, and seemingly lifeless. It was about as lackluster as UMB-2, only untouched by human greed. On a mass scale, anyway. Cauldron Quarry was the lone exception.

"It's about to get funner," Roy said, almost hanging up on the word. He cleared his throat. "Nessa, come up and launch Dewey."

Donnie perked up in his seat. He had not realized her *Lancer* was fitted with a DWE-2L. Colloquially called "Dewey" by pilots across the galaxy, the DWE was a mobile spy-drone capable of providing closed-circuit aerial surveillance in the field. The *detachable wingless explorer* was the second iteration of the base model; the 2L was a lightweight version that provided improved maueverability compared to its predecessors.

"Firing him up," Nessa muttered, flipping switches. "And…launching."

The other pilots turned their Mechs toward her *Lancer*. From under the armored T-shaped antenna protruding from the Mech's upper back emerged this drone. It was a dome-shaped device, like an incomplete light bulb, about the size of a large man's torso. It fluttered into the air, gained elevation, and then glided toward the ridge at ten kilometers-an-hour.

"Altitude?" Roy asked, a moment before the video feed synchronized with everyone's Mechs, thanks to Nessa.

"Twenty meters."

"Give us a broader view. Increase to forty."

"Copy. Remember, gets fuzzy at fifty."

"I know."

Nessa complied, piloting the drone via a thumb-operated analog stick protruding from her seat's left armrest.

As it went higher, the DWE-2L passed over the ridge, and a few reactions briefly muddied their com-link. Kit failed to suppress an audible gasp; Roy mumbled "fuckin' hell," and Wyatt let out a low, hoarse "I'll be damned."

Every reaction was valid. Though Donnie and Nessa were silent at first, they sweated no less.

6

A drop in the terrain about five-hundred meters past the ridge was apparent from the drone's perspective. Cauldron Quarry. The Ferrocore contract had provided an estimated diameter of half a kilometer; at its narrowest, two-hundred meters. This part of the quarry allegedly rose to a point, allowing Mechs and vehicles to drive in and out of the manmade crater.

From the quarry emerged two pillars of smoke.

Directly beneath the drone, however, more alarming sights were beheld.

"Slowing down, providing enhancements," Nessa said, and gulped. She decelerated the drone, then dialed in some magnification on select points of interest.

The ridge demarcated the end of lifeless ochre desert, and the beginning of an arid steppe. Leafless thickets populated the whitish-brown, flat terrain, but not en masse. Across an expanse of several acres in the immediate vicinity, there were maybe thirty. Each shrub no larger than an electric coupe.

There was one in particular that stole their attention above the rest, mainly because it was accompanied by a parachute. It looked like a cloud that had fallen from the sky, partially draping the thicket. Spiny limbs poked at it from below, but not enough to penetrate the white poly-Kevlar. Its cords were still attached to the ejection seat of a Mech, twelve feet away, a bottom corner lodged in the dry earth.

Minus the pilot.

Nessa spun the drone around, sweeping its vantage point in search of a body.

Nothing.

"Focus on the Mech, sis," Roy said.

Nessa complied, and navigated the drone forty meters ahead. The machine from which the seat had been ejected, according to a gaping cockpit and detached canopy lying on the ground fifty feet away, was a red and black *Adder*.

"Well…that ain't good." Donnie's heart sank a little. The *Adder* wasn't a common model by any means, and it took a considerably competent pilot to helm one effectively.

Even if it was technically an enemy machine, seeing it out of commission like this was a little disheartening. Not unlike witnessing the death of your doppelgänger.

All the more unnerving were the circumstances.

Nobody addressed it yet, but everyone was thinking about it. The contract had been signed over to the Mud Wolves, an addendum made to include the Twin Dragons. Theoretically, other mercs could visit the site but not hijack the contract, as most big bounties weren't paid in cash.

There was no reason any of the Mechs on-planet, much less so close to Cauldron Quarry, should be in this condition.

"Is it Starchitect?" Kit asked. "Can you tell?"

"Even if it *is* part of their security team," Wyatt said, "they may not share insignia."

"True," Roy echoed, with a caveat. "But most high-end employers will still slap a decal on the leg."

"Either way," Nessa said, "we won't be seeing the front of its legs from here. Poor bastard's face-down. Pilot must've ejected last-second."

"Uh…I hate to admit this out loud, but…"

Donnie's voice trailed off, and the emptiness on their com-link that followed led everyone but Nessa to turn their Mechs toward his *Adder*.

Inside, Donnie's gaze was glued to Dewey's video feed, studying the fallen Mech.

"There is no damage to the posterior armor," he finally said. "No Laser burns, plasma residue, ballistic powder—*nothing*. Not even small-arms fire or BFT."

The only blunt-force trauma that could visibly damage a Mech's armor, even on its weaker backside, was structural. Collision with another Mech at increased speed, or the collapse of a building.

At any rate, the other pilots saw that—with Nessa's assistance, magnifying the drone's view of the fallen *Adder*—he was right. No indication of enemy weapons damage, or environmental for that matter.

"Why the ejection, then?" Kit asked.

"Got me," Wyatt said.

Hearing sheer puzzlement from the oldest and most experienced one among them wasn't comforting.

Roy's *Kodiak* took three strides toward the ridge, only the tops of his square missile racks peering over it. His cockpit view was still blocked by the slight incline of the hardened ochre plain.

"Are we advancing?" Nessa asked.

"Keep Dewey in the air," Roy said. "But stay on the ridge. Just enough to clear it with your arms."

"Copy. What are you thinking?"

"I want an IR scan."

"I second that," Donnie said, advancing to stand twenty meters to Roy's right.

"Solid," Roy said. "Kit, take my eight. How's your Sub-TD?"

"Active and underappreciated."

"Good, let's put her to work. Wyatt? You mind hanging back again?"

"I don't need babysitting," Nessa sighed.

"How's a wingman then?" Wyatt suggested. "At least until the coast is clear, then Roy can fill my boots."

"Can't argue," Nessa said, after a long pause.

"Alright, let's hit it." Roy pushed his *Kodiak* forward, up the ridge. "Slow and steady, wide POV."

Donnie stayed at his three o'clock, while Kit maintained his back left flank. They summited the ridge, and crossed it without a single misstep. The three-toed feet of avian-legged Mechs like the *Kodiak* and *Adder* made them nimbler than their masses suggested. Though more humanoid in form, including its legs, Kit's *Shieldmaiden* had particularly versatile feet to accompany its Middleweight agility.

"IR's rebooting, targeting sensors just fluttered again," Roy said, and his *Kodiak* came to a stop fifty meters from the ejection seat. He cursed under his breath, which their comms barely picked up. "Gotta be a jammer nearby, or something."

"Outskirts of the quarry, would make sense, defensively," Donnie said. He halted his *Adder* to maintain Roy's right flank. The Mech's rotund torso spun left and right, slowly and methodically, his gaze studious of the open environment.

"Sit tight, Sub-TD is scanning," Kit added, advancing a mere three steps.

The *Shieldmaiden*'s subterranean threat-detection system was standard on Lightweight and Middleweight Mechs, given their common role as sentries. The Sub-TD patent had originally been abbreviated to STD, but that didn't take long for Ursa Steel's developers to change.

Much like the system itself, which utilized proximity LiDAR and subatomic EMP waves to detect explosive devices such as IEDs and landmines. Effective within a forty-meter radius, readings could be provided in under ten seconds.

"All clear," Kit said, eight seconds later.

"Copy," Roy said.

"Color me relieved," Donnie said. "Roy, how's that IR looking? Mine had trouble starting. Reboot just finished."

"Weird. But yeah, it's up now. Sweeping."

The *Kodiak*'s anterior infrared sensors scanned the area, as far as a hundred meters in front of the Mech. Only semisolid objects such as foliage and fabric can be penetrated by the sensors. Transmitters of increased heat, like Mechs and vehicles, can be read through most walls.

Obviously, the latter didn't apply to their current situation. However—

"I've got faint thermals behind this shrub," Roy said, his voice tensing. The *Kodiak*'s torso turned slightly to the right, and then bowed a minor ten degrees. An IR laser exclusively visible to the other pilots appeared on their HUDs, linking his right-arm Autocannon to a thicket twenty meters away.

It was about that same distance from the one draped by the parachute, which was almost within arm's reach of the *Kodiak*'s left foot.

"Permission to flank left," Kit said, to nobody in particular but assuming Roy as their current leader. Donnie had no qualms with this, in situations like these it was fair to share the vanguard role, and unless someone objected, whoever answered first was kosher.

"Granted, but hold your fire," Roy replied, giving a mere two-second pause for Donnie's sake. Hearing no objections increased Roy's respect for him.

"Copy. Moving."

The *Shieldmaiden* performed a crescent maneuver, circling around the left flank of the steppe before them. Nessa began to say something, Wyatt's own heavy breathing palpable over their comms, when the thicket shuddered.

Roy's heat reading flared.

And, Nessa's drone continuing to hover, relayed the motion, too.

A pilot, on foot, emerged from behind the shrub. It was a woman, half of whose face was a bright blue, and the same lambent fluid splattered the top of her jumpsuit. Instead of reaching for, or wielding a weapon, she held her hands high above her head. A ubiquitous gesture of surrender.

Only Roy and Donnie were close enough, to see through their canopies, the undeniable look of fear and disquiet on the pilot's face. Not the fear of being captured by an enemy force, though, nor the dread of death at the "hands" of a Mech.

This was different.

"She's surrendering. And Starchitect confirmed." Roy tutted. "See the patch on her left shoulder?"

Donnie enhanced his optics.

"I see it. That's them, alright. Security detail."

The patch was a white star whose upper point was fashioned into a steeple.

"What's the move?" Wyatt asked.

"You two, summit the ridge and hold, for overwatch." Roy sighed. "I don't like this. And the smoke coming from the quarry doesn't help."

Everyone's silence spoke volumes of agreement.

Nessa's *Lancer* and Wyatt's imposing *Raider* proceeded forward, pausing at the peak of the ridgeline behind the other Mechs. Their movement caught the enemy pilot's attention. She turned, jerkily, and craned her head back slightly to witness their manifestation.

"She's scared shitless. Shaking, even." Donnie felt a chill, as if it came out of the blue. He flipped a toggle on his dash, leaned forward and typed on a keyboard. "Running vitals."

"I say we leave her," Nessa suggested, coldly but reasonably. "Prioritize the quarry."

"Juggling it," Roy muttered.

"We should cuff her, just in case, for now," Kit said. Her *Shieldmaiden* gingerly approached. "Then book it to Cauldron."

"At your own risk, but she appears unarmed," Donnie said.

Carefully, minding his footing more than anything, Roy circled the shrub she had been hiding behind, simultaneously stomping the parachute-draped thicket, too.

"I don't see anything, either," Roy added.

"I'm magnified on the seat," Nessa said, eyeing the drone footage. "Her pistol's still in the holster. I bet the Murmur is in the back, too."

"Left in a hurry, did we?" Roy's voice echoed into the open, thanks to a communication channel to the speaker situated on the outside of his Mech.

The woman waved her arms and shouted back, but a howling desert wind muffled her words, compounded by the denseness of their canopies.

"No reason taunting her, dick," Nessa said.

Roy disabled external communications while smirking wryly. The odd intensity of the situation quickly sapped any humor he had mustered, anyway.

"Heartrate is spiked, blood pressure's through the roof, but no foreign bodies or infections," Donnie relayed. "Maybe some shellshock, nothing more."

"What's the blue shit on her?"

"No idea. Maybe they struck oil."

"Alien oil?" Roy scoffed.

"Or blood," Kit said, her voice and heart sinking.

The realization, the possibility, hit them all in staggered waves.

"The theories can wait, I've got a reality check for y'all," Wyatt said, vaulting his voice just shy of shouting it into his mic. "Tracking two enemy Mechs, at the edge of the quarry. Shy of five-hundred meters. Accruing data now."

Everyone suddenly ignored the female pilot's existence. Their Mechs faced the direction of the quarry, easily designated by the flowing columns of smoke in bright daylight.

"Shit." There was so much palpable stress in Wyatt's single syllable. Then another, followed by two words no pilot wanted to hear, especially at this range. "Fuck. Tracking a *Gunslinger* and an *Onslaught*. One each."

Donnie's heart sank.

His mind raced. Why would Starchitect have employed an *Onslaught* for a *mining* compound? It was the big brother of the *Odin* and *Raider*, a 110-ton monster, and the only Mech ever produced to tip the scales over a hundred. It was also ten feet taller than both

Mechs, reaching sixty off the ground. Its potential armaments alone were unnervingly daunting.

"Fall in, fall in!" Roy declared, advancing past the face-down *Adder*. His own targeting system remained glitchy, but was beginning to process data from the distant enemy Mechs. Or attempting to. "Fuck! My TAC is still misbehaving. Kit, scan for a jammer in the vicinity. Something's gotta be—"

"Did and done, there's nothing here."

"Nothing within the radius of your Sub-TD, and what's that, fifty meters?" Nessa said, almost sneering with skepticism. She wasn't mad *at* Kit, just their situation and the fact that an *Onslaught* was downrange.

"Forty," Kit corrected, unenthusiastically.

"Jammers don't have a range beyond that, anyway," Donnie said. His voice went hoarse. "Unless Fleet equipment."

"Starchitect is a long ways from Fleet."

Roy had a good point, but that didn't change the fact that their targeting systems were awry and the mining company had employed an imposing security detail. One that seemed unnecessary, or overkill, given the region.

His last statement had been even and collected. A casual statement. The next time Roy spoke, there was a burst of panic, and amid the three words he exclaimed, a distinct alarm sounded in the background.

"Fuck! I'm painted!"

The *Kodiak* immediately began to move, breaking formation in a zigzag pattern. The Mech's avian legs and pronged feet gave it higher mobility than most Mechs its size. The *Adder* was its only match in that department.

"Gotta be that *Onslaught*," Nessa growled, advancing from the front of the ridge.

"Scatter, we've got 'em beat in numbers," Donnie snapped. "Wyatt, push forward. The *second* your TAC lights up, paint the *Onslaught* and launch a flight."

"Copy."

The Mud Dragons, as it were, moved collectively, albeit in a seemingly formless maneuver.

Only Kit remained, the least active, as she harbored some incredulity about the *Adder*'s pilot. Amid the panic of the others, the woman had gone unnoticed. Kit spotted her reach the ejection seat, and withdraw the SBR from the back compartment.

"Our pilot's officially armed, not that it matters much to us," Kit informed the others.

"You're right, it doesn't," Wyatt said. He was throttling his *Raider* in hopes of achieving better range for his missiles, while furiously rebooting his TAC.

"An Imperator might annoy your canopy," Donnie said. "But a Murmur won't do shit. Ignore her. On us, Kit."

"Ugh, copy."

She wasn't happy about it, but complied anyway. Good points were made like common sense. She followed that.

"Missiles in the air, anyone else painted?" Roy asked, his *Kodiak* still slaloming. He had muted his alarms, but the flashing red light couldn't be turned off. He was being targeted by the *Onslaught*, a flight of its LRMs coursing through the desert air. The swarm of six 50mm missiles had about 470 meters to travel, arcing up before theorctically pummeling the target. They led a flare of white flame propulsion, followed by contrails snaking across the near cloudless sky.

"Negative," his comrades sounded off.

Until Wyatt's *Raider* was within the *Onslaught*'s own impressive TAC range, Roy's *Kodiak* was the only prominent enough heat source to be targeted at this distance. It seemed that the humanoid behemoth that was the *Onslaught* didn't have any interest in advancing. Whereas its wingman, a twin-barreled *Gunslinger*, was rapidly approaching. The squat Middleweight was similar to a *Brawler* in mass, but its two arms, composed of startlingly long cannons, made the *Gunslinger* a much greater threat in long-distance engagements.

Roy had armed his MiDS, a rudimentary missile-deterrent system consisting of a turret mounted between his shoulder racks. The turret emerged from a dome covering when armed, and operated automatically. It was a basic "spray and pray" system, one that had a 70% success rate for missiles within twenty meters.

Fortunately, this was one of those cases.

Three of the six warheads caught the turret's hose of 10mm bullets, detonating eighteen meters from the *Kodiak*'s cockpit. The explosions consumed and destroyed the other three missiles. Roy's canopy rattled and his heat levels spiked a meager 8% before relief fell over him.

"Threat eliminated," Roy sighed. "For now."

Forty meters behind them, Kit was playing catch-up. She had about passed the fallen *Adder* when she noticed movement through her canopy and flinched, stopping the *Shieldmaiden* in its tracks.

The face-down *Adder* appeared completely intact and almost devoid of damage. Its torso was only slightly turned to the side, the cockpit's nose half-buried in the ground, its narrow canopy now just a slit of an opening where the ejection had occurred.

She stared at it from her own cockpit, studying the machine for signs of life. The abandoned Mech budged again, as if it was trying to stand. Once more Kit flinched, and impulsively gripped his weapons stick.

"Uh, guys," Kit said, worriedly. "The enemy *Adder* is moving."

"It's *what*?" Wyatt asked, his face scrunching.

The distinctive vents composing its broad shoulders, used to dump heat from mounted cannons, suddenly poured something organic. Kit's expression distorted. Like massive orange tapeworms, some kind of ophidian creature slithered between the slatted openings.

"You're seeing things, Kit," Roy insisted. "I'm being painted again, though, and that's a reality. Can someone light up this *Onslaught*? I don't care if you're out of range, just do *something*."

Everyone but Kit saw the new flight of LRMs arcing into the air, about four-hundred meters away. Below their trajectory advanced the *Gunslinger*, which finally began to represent its name. The cannon-arms varied Mech to Mech, depending on the pilot and a number of other situations. They could be Autocannons, coilguns, or even rotaries.

This one had a pair of Gauss rifles, colloquially referred as coilguns, utilizing electromagnetic capacitors. When the *Gunslinger* fired both simultaneously, twin trails of warped oxygen followed the 200mm disc-shaped tungsten projectiles toward their target. Thrice the speed of any energy-based weapon, but 40% slower than any caliber AC. The enemy's first shots missed Nessa's *Lancer* moments after she had started zigzagging. They had come so close, straying a ten feet from her left arm, that she could sense a vibration in her cockpit.

Behind Kit, the slugs walloped the ridge they had previously passed over. Had it not been for the ridge, they would have continued for another few hundred meters.

"Fuck me, I was hoping for ACs," Nessa said.

Even 90mm Autocannons, which would be terminally devastating to a Middleweight if the angle was right, weren't as unnerving as coilguns. A well-placed slug could sever a completely healthy limb, or penetrate the armor shrouding a Mech's engine.

Donnie had started putting shots downrange, targeting the *Onslaught*. His medium-bore Lasers stabbed green light in its direction, but he was out of effective range, so they dissipated before reaching it. Still, they seemed to get the pilot's attention, and within seconds he was being painted by its LRMs.

"Missiles locked," he announced, alarms briefly blaring around him. He muted them. "I hope you're happy, Roy."

"Let 'em come, just keep dancing," Roy said. "Tell him, Nessa, ain't nobody this side of the galaxy better than me at shooting down LRMs."

"He's right, Donnie. And he's not talking about the turret."

The *Onslaught* launched another cluster of six LRMs. The group of Mechs had gradually proceeded across the steppe, nearing the quarry slowly but surely. The distance between them and the *Onslaught* was now within three-hundred meters.

"Big as that sumbitch is," Wyatt added, "he's only got four flights left, if I'm right."

The *Onslaught* had a single shoulder-mounted rack about the size of an *Odin*'s, flush with its head-like cockpit. Most of its imposing weapons systems were arm and torso-mounted.

"Then maybe we drain it," Roy suggested.

"Incoming!" Donnie exclaimed, and thrusted his mouthpiece in.

An artificial lightning bolt of blue plasma suddenly stabbed at Roy's *Kodiak*, hitting it in the left shoulder. He shook in his seat as the cockpit rocked side to side, blue light obscuring his canopy. He had just lined up his shots to target the incoming missiles.

Firing blind, he squeezed a trigger and jabbed a stud simultaneously. Cheek-mounted machineguns punched the sky with .50-caliber rounds, accompanied by a pair of large-bored lasers. The red lances streaked the plummeting missiles, but only one was caught in its path. It exploded, engulfing two others. His machinegun rounds missed, and the remaining three warheads hailed Donnie's *Adder*.

Two impacted his left shoulder, detonating in "small" red fireballs, each the size of a car. He had still been moving, and wasn't about to stop, Donnie's sweaty hand maintaining a grip on the throttle. His right hand, however, slipped free of the joystick, and his torso locked center. Paired with the detonations engulfing the *Adder*'s left shoulder, Donnie was nearly shaken from his seat. The harness held him in place, bruising his shoulders and ribs.

His helmet would have flung off had his right hand not managed to catch it in time.

Of the trio that survived Roy's makeshift countermeasures, blinded by the *Onslaught*'s PPC strike, only two made it to Donnie. The third hit dirt, blasting a divot of scorched terrain into the steppe behind the *Adder*'s left foot.

"Two's better than six, how you doing, Donnie?" Roy asked, suppressing his own frustration. His TAC was temporarily fried, his entire HUD distorted from the brief EMP effects of the PPC.

"Just a scratch," Donnie said, a bit muffled at first. Then he spit out his mouthpiece. "Armor's at ninety-two."

Roy could barely hear Donnie's pain, which spoke volumes of his tenacity as a pilot and a leader.

"Sorry 'bout that, fucker blindsided me—literally—with a PPC."

"Let's return the favor, then, shall we?" Donnie had caught his breath, wiped his sweaty right hand on his jumpsuit, and returned it to the textured grip of the joystick. "My TAC is up and running, again."

"Solid copy. Wyatt?"

"We've got a worse problem than the *Onslaught*." Words nobody wanted to hear, especially in his voice.

"Come again," Nessa said, still mobile but curving around and rotating her torso to face their six.

Wyatt's *Raider* had halted and dared put its back to the enemy Mechs in favor of assisting Kit.

"Well, maybe not *worse*," he added. "But definitely more disconcerting."

7

Kit was grateful that Wyatt saw it, too. That she wasn't hallucinating. The two tapeworm-like creatures that had slithered through the *Adder*'s vents to coil around its shoulders were at least sixty feet long. Much like how a human's intestines were fifteen feet long, it stunned Kit to imagine that the alien snakes had managed to stay hidden inside the *Adder*.

Ironically appropriate, albeit.

The creatures' length and movement were snake-like, but that was where the similarities ended. Though limbless, they were almost completely flat but sported a strange hammerhead-like crest at the end of their snouts. These spanned five or six feet, just slightly broader than the creature's body width, and were a dull gray hue contrary to their rust-colored skin.

"Alien contact, from the *Adder*," Kit said, flipping switches on the control panel above her. "Recording feed now. In case Ferrocore plays the clueless card."

"Good idea," Wyatt said, and began to record his own feed.

"Nessa, get Dewey's eyes on the *Adder* so we can all see what the fuck's going on. Not that our hands aren't full as it is."

"On it," Nessa replied, almost robotically.

"Seems they were inside all along," Kit thought out loud.

"No wonder she bailed," Wyatt said.

The pilot, though armed, now hunkered down behind her ejection seat. She used it as cover, although the creatures didn't seem to possess any kind of ranged attack. They also just slithered there, around the decommissioned *Adder*, like maggots squirming in a carcass.

"Are they posing a threat?" Donnie asked, his mouthpiece dangling from the neckline of his jumpsuit.

"Not really," Kit said, through a grimace as she continued to study the creatures.

"Good, because the Mechs are." Attitude in Donnie's voice, albeit understandably. "And we need your help."

"But boss—" Kit began.

"Now, goddammit!" Donnie snapped. "Kit, we need your mobility. Distract the *Gunslinger*, maybe he's dumb enough to think he can actually track you with his Gauss. Wyatt. *Wyatt*! We need your firepower, old man."

"On my way."

"Hold up!" Kit said, spotting something of greater interest.

Donnie muttered an expletive.

Another PPC strike from the *Onslaught*, and although it missed both Donnie and Roy, whose Mechs were now but a mere twenty meters apart, the plasma fried the air between them. Their HUDs and TAC systems fluttered.

"They're like huge tapeworms," Kit said.

"I know, I see 'em on Dewey's feed."

"They've got horns, or crests, whatever," Kit continued. "They're *sparking*, Donnie."

"They're *what*?" Roy asked, back to moving again. Toward the quarry, giving the enemy Mechs a wide berth, though the *Gunslinger* now seemed intent on pursuing Nessa. He glanced at his visor-displayed drone feed, but couldn't discern the details that Kit described.

From the *Shieldmaiden*'s cockpit, optics enhanced on her HUD, Kit inspected the creatures' rounded snouts. The hammerhead stone-like crests were sparking white arcs, some kind of charged current.

"Maybe that's what's jamming our equipment," she suggested.

"That's insane," Nessa said. "That's literally—"

"She might be right," Roy said. "My TAC is good as new, now that I'm far enough from the *Adder*. Donnie, too."

"Same," Wyatt said.

Kit checked her own systems. Her HUD alone was still a flickering mess.

"Can confirm, I'm still in its range."

"Well, good to know," Donnie said. "Now play tomato or I'll squish you myself if we make it out of this."

Kit couldn't help but smirk, and then she complied. But as she turned her Mech away from the *Adder*, the rotary Autocannon that composed her left arm rattled off two-dozen shots in the blink of an eye. The volley of 20mm rounds skittered across the *Adder*'s backside, shredding the serpentine creatures in the process. She observed their condition via her rear camera.

One appeared dead, limp like a warm noodle.

The other still moved, and it seemed that Kit's action had stirred something in the pilot. She emerged from behind the seat to engage the creature forty meters away, yelling and firing once within range of the SBR. The creature hissed, spittle spraying from its fanged mouth, and bullets significantly smaller than Kit's RAC pummeled its skin.

Kit didn't have time to hang around.

She wished the pilot good luck, but had bigger fish to fry. She drove her *Shieldmaiden* toward the battle downrange, recalling Donnie's planned strategy of distracting the *Gunslinger*. Which, she noticed, was currently dancing around Nessa.

Wyatt had also rejoined the fight.

He sent an imposing flight of twelve LRMs once his TAC had locked onto the *Onslaught*. He suspected at least half of them would be shot down, but if six made impact, it was a tiny victory. Of course, the outlandish armor protection that the superior Mech carried would make the hits seem trivial at best. The only benefit to hitting the *Onslaught* with a few fireballs was momentarily obstructing its pilot's view. And possibly distracting it from the others.

Wyatt was ready to go toe-to-toe with the *Onslaught*, especially knowing he had the support of such proficient pilots.

A quartet of red Lasers reached Roy, but only two hit. The third and fourth missed by mere feet. The two that did impact didn't hold for longer than a split-second, searing armor but not doing much else. He was maintaining a good level of speed, with erratic footwork and torso-swinging, to avoid catching any direct hits from the *Onslaught*.

Meanwhile, Donnie was charging the massive Mech, more in hopes of getting within its missiles' minimum range than draining its reserves.

Magnifying his optics, now at 220 meters, he could see the *Onslaught*'s right abdominal barrel flicker blue. Charged white-hot arcs gained color as the PPC prepared to fire. It was a quick process, but not as instantaneous as a regular Laser or any ballistic weapon for that matter. An experienced and keen enough pilot as Donnie could anticipate a PPC under the right conditions.

The clear skies and relatively unsullied desert air provided them.

When the PPC discharged, Donnie's linear bumrush feinted. He sidestepped, dodging the massive blast of charged particles. His HUD and TAC flickered, but reformed in two seconds. Then he threw his own assault at the stationary Mech. Like a humanoid golem of ferrosteel with a fusion heart, the jungle-green *Onslaught* was an imposing sight to anyone in the galaxy.

Pilot, soldier, civilian.

No matter their experience in combat.

However—it also made for a very easy target. Tall, broad-shouldered, and lumbering. Its maximum speed was 70% that of a *Raider*'s, and it took a good while to accelerate.

Donnie's *Adder* had twin shoulder-mounted Gauss rifles. He utilized them. The coilguns fired, leaving pale green trails of disturbed atoms in their wake. Both converged on the *Onslaught* just as it began to move. Two disc-like tungsten slugs shore through the outer armor on the Mech's robust left hip. It didn't falter the slightest, but any amount of damage was something to put on the board.

Donnie adjusted his aim higher, and continued his charge.

A cluster of four large-bore Lasers stabbed at Donnie from the *Onslaught*'s right breast. Three of them caught his *Adder*'s left shoulder. Previously damaged armor from the LRMs melted away, and heat bombarded the Mech's ventilation system. An ironic conflict that vaulted his levels to 77%, paired with fleeting alarms.

"Coming around, Donnie, at your four o'clock," Roy announced. "You brave, crazy son of a bitch."

Donnie smirked. He spotted the *Kodiak* pass the periphery of his rear camera, and then returned his full attention to the *Onslaught*. Although it was trying to make haste away from the quarry and toward its comrade, which still danced and exchanged shots with Nessa, the behemoth wasn't getting away. Donnie closed the space between them, and before five seconds had transpired he was just under a hundred meters away.

Meanwhile, Kit was providing effective distraction for the *Gunslinger*. Its torso swung to and fro, firing one coilgun at Nessa's *Lancer*, and then its other at the *Shieldmaiden*, missing both.

"This asshole thinks he can catch us," Nessa smirked devilishly. "Let's put him in a lasso."

"Copy," Kit said, sneering at the brown and green *Gunslinger* with angry resolution.

To Mech pilots, a lasso was a maneuver ideal for two-to-one odds, though at greater ranges as many as four could be on the outside. Those with greater numbers ran circles around their target, which had many benefits. It tended to dizzy the pilot, induce the fear of defeat, and draw him or her to build heat or waste ammo by firing; most of their shots, depending on the speed of the runners, wouldn't land.

All the while their Mech's legs were being hit with salvo after salvo. This, as opposed to focusing on the enemy's torso, eliminated potential crossfire.

Theoretically, the *Gunslinger* could eject or gesture surrender. The latter typically entailed pointing its weapons skyward, or at the ground.

Instead, the *Gunslinger*'s pilot kept pivoting on its blocky feet, thirteen-foot Gauss barrels swinging with it. Occasionally their muzzles flashed white-green and a slug would miss its target. Nessa's *Lancer* was far from nimble, but with Kit's help their maneuver proved that the *Gunslinger* pilot was too grin for the situation.

A competent machinehead would have stayed in place and anticipated the *Lancer* every time it came around.

Meanwhile the *Gunslinger*'s stocky legs endured sloughs of melted armor. Nessa kept hitting it with her four medium Lasers, each one leaving a green scar in the ferrosteel. Whereas Kit favored her right-arm PPC, but due to the heat production and recharge rate, periodically cycled her own two medium Lasers.

Together, they had brought the *Gunslinger*'s leg armor integrity down to 40% in under a minute.

Another few well-placed hits and it would have nowhere to go but down.

Then its torso pitched back, barrels aimed at the sky.

"He's surrendering," Kit said.

"Damn!" Nessa spat. "I really wanted to cripple this bastard."

Kit sighed and, with Nessa, stopped in her tracks. She strode right past the *Gunslinger*, which ironically was doing a cliché act from western films of old.

Reach for the sky!

This made Kit smirk, though it dissolved when she witnessed what Donnie was doing. Charging the *Onslaught*, which was now backpedaling in her direction, but turning to face Roy's *Kodiak*. Toward the smoking quarry.

She saw a horde of red Lasers streak across the hundred-meter gap between Roy and the enemy Mech, likely belonging to both of them. An exchange of shots, but what landed she couldn't tell. Donnie's *Adder* fired at the *Onslaught*, his twin shoulder-mounted coilguns zipping through the air and walloping the *Onslaught* center-mass. As Kit advanced, she saw a crescent shard of armor, at least three feet long, fly off the behemoth's torso.

"On your six," she heard Nessa say.

Kit's confidence returned.

Behind them, Wyatt fired a warning shot at the *Gunslinger*'s feet. Accepting surrenders given the circumstances probably wasn't in their best interest; they couldn't babysit the enemy until the job was done. Everyone was needed to neutralize the *Onslaught*, and then investigate the quarry. Putting their backs to the *Gunslinger* and its massive coilguns wasn't wise, but right now they would have to manage.

Donnie gnawed on his mouthpiece and growled through his shielded teeth as he neared the towering *Onslaught*. Sunlight peered over its broad shoulders, and an imposing shadow blanketed Donnie's canopy.

Its LRMs were of no use now.

He armed his SRMs, their shorter range requiring no lock-on. Chest-mounted, the six-missile rack fired like a load of buckshot, but packed with small metal-composite warheads. Each one-third the yield of an LRM, but still effective within sixty meters.

Donnie was half that.

He thumbed his firing stud and the unguided missiles shot out of their pods with a crisp boom. They struck their target, small fireballs blossoming together under the *Onslaught*'s right abdomen. Its left-arm AC couldn't reach him, though despite his proximity, the Mech's torso was still spun to engage Roy.

Donnie skirted to the *Onslaught*'s right, the top of his *Adder* barely reaching the behemoth's "stomach." Where, on either side, its PPC cannons were mounted. The enemy pilot fired them both simultaneously, the brunt of their energy missing him and emptying down-range, but the muzzle-spray still frazzled his electronics. Donnie's HUD sputtered and his TAC had a seizure.

The *Adder*'s heat levels skyrocketed.

Inside the cockpit, between and below its shoulders, Donnie sweated. More than before.

"Fucker," he growled through his mouthpiece.

Downrange from the *Onslaught*, his back to the quarry, Roy minded the *Adder* as he returned fire. Only one of the enemy's PPC lances had hit home. And not a direct impact, either. The splash of azure energy rocked his cockpit and disoriented his HUD. Roy's dark skin gleamed with sweat and reflected the red light of heat alarms that bathed his cockpit crimson.

Despite the disorientation of his TAC, he still managed to line up his Autocannons. The two arm-mounted weapons discharged on-target. A pair of 60mm rounds caught the *Onslaught* in the chest, producing a plume of sparks and white flame.

"Roy!" Donnie shouted. "Concentrate fire on the abdomen. See if we can overheat the PPCs."

"Solid copy," Roy chimed, continuing to circle around the *Onslaught*. It ignored Donnie's presence, because it really had no choice. Its PPCs could continue to disorient his systems, but cause no real damage. The breast-mounted lasers and arm-AC couldn't reach him at all. The *Onslaught*'s right arm ended in a humanoid fist that could be used to strike an enemy Mech, destroy a building, or clear a path of debris.

The *Adder* was just under its reach.

The *Kodiak*, however…

Roy wouldn't be getting that close. It was already one hell of a risk for Donnie. Worst-case, he could crouch his Mech at the cost of moving slower, but clear the *Onslaught*'s PPC EMP spray, and absolutely avoid that fist.

A sudden barrage of ballistic fire slammed into the *Onslaught*'s backside, from Donnie's seven o'clock. He glimpsed his rear camera and spotted two Mechs advancing, about 140 meters out. Kit led, her *Shieldmaiden*'s RAC spinning and spewing. The rotary variant was faster than any other Autocannon, capable of chewing through the armor on lighter Mechs and crippling with the right aim. For a monster like the *Onslaught*, it sufficed to annoy it and rally the pilot's attention.

Perhaps foolish to turn its back on a *Kodiak*, the merc pivoted the giant Mech's feet to face their other attackers. Kit veered left, RAC still spinning. She periodically let out her twin Lasers, dragging green beams of heat across its torso.

Nessa, having heard Donnie's plan, focused on the *Onslaught*'s abdominal particle cannons. The massive chrome barrels, their muzzles darkened with smolder burns, were hard to miss. Nessa's quartet of large-bore Lasers fixated on them, trying to target their openings. Easier said than done, but it was a worthy challenge.

Donnie began to backpedal, now, facing the *On-slaught*'s right hip. He hammered home another blast of SRMs, slamming into the side of its right PPC. Both of them suddenly flashed blue, and Kit managed to evade one by about thirty feet. Nessa tried to, but her *Lancer* was too slow. A blast of charged plasma engulfed her left arm, and vaulted her heat levels to 80%, nullifying the use of her Lasers until it dropped.

"Locking on, drop back, Donnie," Roy said.

"Negative, negative!" Donnie rattled off. "Focus fire on the midsection. Let's try to overwhelm the capacitors."

Big as the PPC mounts were, it was feasible.

Especially with the *Onslaught* so outnumbered. Wyatt periodically checked his rear camera to confirm the stagnancy of the *Gunslinger*. To his surprise, the pilot was playing true to their surrender. If he or she were to abandon that and fire upon them again, whether in the back or face-to-face, their opportunity was forfeit. By code, their enemy was *encouraged* to destroy them.

"Copy, concentrating fire, but still, put some more space between you two," Roy said.

"Not too much, or that massive AC will lobotomize me."

"Understood."

Donnie backpedaled another twenty or thirty feet, while his Gauss rifles fixated on the right PPC mount. The tungsten slugs didn't do much to the actual barrels, but the surrounding armor was disintegrating rapidly. As hot as PPCs could get, especially a dual system, heatsinks were often mounted in the immediate area. If they could damage a few of them, more than half the battle was already won.

"I'm painted, I'm painted, *fuck*!" Kit suddenly exclaimed, and began zigzagging as if a fifty-ton gazelle.

"Stop juking and charge the bastard, Kit!"

Realizing her error, and the merit of Donnie's strategy, she did just that. Her *Shieldmaiden* was the only Mech present that could halve a hundred meters sooner than the *Onslaught*'s six LRMs would reach her. No more than two seconds after cutting that distance, the minimum range of the enemy missiles, they battered the ground behind her. The Elnath steppe gave way to a twenty-meter crater as the warheads detonated. Kit rocked in her seat from the vibrations, but no more than a breath of heat splashed the back of her Mech's torso.

Everyone in their crew immediately lost any iota of respect for the *Onslaught* pilot. Going after Kit like that, realizing their defeat, the merc figured they'd take out the most susceptible target before it was over.

Roy hammered four consecutive shots from his 60mm Autocannons. They clustered around the *Onslaught*'s midsection, and according to his TAC, the massive Mech's armor integrity in that region was down to 33%, though the rest of its body was well above eighty.

Kit's response was an angry jab of Lasers overlapped by the pounding precision of her RAC. Having to aim slightly up at the *Onslaught* given their height differences, there was zero risk of crossfire with Donnie on the other side. Though he was beginning to put more distance between them, while simultaneously pivoting to get a better angle on its right PPC.

Facing the *Shieldmaiden*, their giant enemy's torso bowed as far as it could to throw a quartet of large-bore Lasers at it. Kit juked and raised her Mech's left arm at the same time, the RAC shielded on the outside by a protruding segment of armor—per its namesake. Two of the *Onslaught*'s Lasers struck the pristine shield, searing into armor but far from penetrating it. The other two beams of red heat went high, one just barely scoring the top of Kit's cockpit-head, and the second missing entirely.

Her heat levels steadied around 60%, which was manageable.

Roy landed a PPC blow into its midsection, Donnie's 90mm ACs slammed four rounds into its right particle cannon mount, and Nessa—having risked greater proximity—battered the area with a blast from her LBX. Were it not for the rattling of his own cockpit from the AC, Donnie would've heard the LBX cluster gnash into the *Onslaught*'s damaged armor.

What he did hear, though, what the entire crew caught, was Wyatt's voice growling through the radio silence. It seemed he had not forgiven the enemy pilot for impudently targeting Kit.

"Fucker. Pick on someone your own size."

Both of the *Raider*'s massive arm-barrels sparked blue before discharging. The PPCs were 20mm larger than Roy's, yielding more energy and greater range. They slashed the air thirty feet to Nessa's left, and she immediately threw the *Lancer* into reverse. The PPC strikes reached the *Onslaught* and devoured its midsection in azure plasma, sloughing armor and annihilating a pair of heatsinks in its abdomen. The right PPC mount flashed white, and Kit aggressively backpedaled as she witnessed the internal explosion. Capacitors inside the weapon overheated and combusted less than two seconds since Wyatt's blow. The blast engulfed the *Onslaught*'s midsection, and when the flames dissipated amid a nimbus of blue-tinged black smoke, the true damage was realized.

It looked as though a massive shark had taken a bite out of the 110-ton Mech's right side. Its torso crumpled in that direction, and the pilot attempted to move the *Onslaught* to the left. Its hip actuator exploded in a spray of sparks, visible through the melted armor, and the Mech collapsed. Its heavy torso met its right leg, the sound alone of mangled armor reaching the cockpits of Nessa and Donnie, those nearest.

Fortunately, they were both far enough away to avoid the collapse.

Nessa had paused her retreat, though, relieved the behemoth had finally been cut down. A smog of dirt still hung in the air around it.

"Excellent work, ladies and gents," Roy said, idling eighty meters away. Sixty meters behind him was the nearest edge of the quarry. He glanced at his rear camera, and the incessant columns of smoke emerging from the pit. "Let's get going. Assemble on me. We need to—"

Nessa's eyes widened and she jerked her throttle back.

"Shit! He's going critical!" Her comms cracked.

"Get outta there!" Donnie shouted, backpedaling himself.

Unlike the nimble *Adder*, the vaguely humanoid *Lancer* was too slow on its feet. An inherent design flaw. The *Onslaught*'s containment coils and the fail-safe system itself must have been damaged during the Mech's defeat. The belated meltdown triggered a radiant white flash, which Nessa caught milliseconds before a spherical explosion devoured the *Onslaught*'s remains. Already on the ground, the blast incurred a stronger shockwave.

Nessa was violently jostled in her seat, harness staying true, and heat warnings blared. Her head throbbed from the sounds and the shaking, sweat dripping from her skin. Damage indicators on her HUD flashed from yellow to red as the shockwave struck the *Lancer*'s legs.

She couldn't hear her brother's voice shouting after her, or her other teammates doing the same. Everything was a mess of static and distortion.

The blast dissipated, more than half of the *Onslaught*'s ruins vaporized. The rest occupied a thirty-meter-wide crater in the Elnath steppe. Nessa regained her composure but felt sick from all the shaking and heat waves.

"…hear me, goddammit…reach you…tight, we're…"

Roy's voice cut in and out of her com-link.

From her teammates' perspective, the dark green and yellow *Lancer* was a harbinger of defeat. Untouched save its bottom half, the armor blackened from heat. Sparks flashed from its knee actuators, which must have been crippled by the shockwave. The Mech was on its last legs, both literally and figuratively.

"Can you move, Nessa?" Wyatt asked.

His own heavy-footed *Raider* lumbered toward them. The crew was assembling on Nessa's position. Roy minded the crater to his right as he passed the enemy's remains en route to his sister.

And then he decelerated, when her voice cut through a burst of static on their frequency. It sputtered briefly before shrugging off any crumb of white noise.

"…just fine, do you read? I can hear you just fine, now. Confirm."

Everyone sounded off.

"Damage report," Roy said, maintain his game-face. Relieved she was uninjured, and even if it was crippled, her Mech was still upright.

"Knee joints are fucked. Picture Wyatt in ten years."

Wyatt smirked. They all did, and Roy shook his head in tandem.

"She won't budge, little brother," Nessa added. "I think the ankles are FUBAR, too."

"Drop the BAR," Donnie said. "I know a techie on Alcor that could fix 'em up for a steal."

"I might have to hold you on that," she replied. "But for now, I don't want to sit out the rest of this contract on my ass. Someone pick me up, if you have room to spare.

"Good looks," Roy said, glancing at the other Mechs. There was only one obvious choice, besides his own. "Wyatt?"

"You got it," he said, and plodded to stand even closer to her immobilized *Lancer*.

"Babysitter duty, huh?" Nessa sighed.

"Negative," Wyatt insisted, detaching his harness to stand. Before removing his helmet, and thus abandoning the com-link, he added: "Prolonging our game of tomato."

They heard his comms click distinctively, confirming that he had broken the channel. They pictured him setting the helmet in his seat, striding to the back of his cockpit, decompressing the hatch, opening it, and casting the composite rope-ladder down the *Raider*'s back.

Nessa had already signed off, shut the *Lancer*'s engine down, and departed her cockpit in the same manner.

Meanwhile, three-hundred meters behind the two Mechs, the Starchitect-employed *Adder* pilot knelt to catch her breath. A bullet-riddled alien lifeform reeked twenty feet away, its vivid blue gore seeping into the otherwise far-from-porous terrain.

"Donnie, Kit," Roy said. "On me. If you don't think we have already, we're gonna go earn the rest of that contract."

"Heard that," Kit said, amassing some morale.

Taking a final glance at Wyatt and Nessa—spotting the latter ascend the back of the *Raider*—Donnie nodded and collected himself, too.

"Let's fucking get it."

8

The trio of Mechs gathered at the edge of an Elnath cliff, where the steppe dropped abruptly. Three-hundred feet below sprawled the ninety-acre Cauldron Quarry, an aggregate pit whose established compound covered maybe three-quarters of the pale, raw terrain. Nearly half of the interconnected buildings had been swallowed by the planet itself, resulting in widespread damage to drilling facilities and solar-powered stations.

Scattered vehicles, from flatbed trucks to tractors and utility carts, arrayed the surrounding terrain. Many of them appeared, at first glance, to be in working condition and merely abandoned.

The two most notable vehicles were a pair of *Tarantulas* in the pit. The unique Mechs were nearly half a kilometer apart, the closest to them at the very base of the cliff they occupied. It was missing two of its four insectoid limbs, tilted to one side at the edge of a small sinkhole. Most machineheads considered the *Tarantula* a hybrid tank than a Mech, given its quadrupedal set-up and mobility. At forty tons it was technically a Lightweight, but its array of armaments, paired with its maneuverability in rough terrain, made it an imposing foe in the right hands.

This one had not been so imposing to whoever—or whatever—it had faced.

A *Tarantula* featured a completely enclosed cockpit to shield the operator, who relied on camera feeds to see. So there was no telling his or her condition, but a shallow halo of smoke did hover around its bulbous torso.

Though nobody discussed it, the crew assumed its operator had died from smoke inhalation or suffocation.

As for the other *Tarantula*—it stood at the far end of the quarry, beside an outbuilding that was likely a fuel depot or waste management. It didn't move, appeared undamaged, and wasn't emitting any heat.

"Could be empty," Donnie suggested.

"Or just…watching. Playing it safe."

"Cauldron's guard-dog," Kit muttered, tacitly seconding Roy's guess.

"Should we fire a warning shot?" Donnie asked. "Maybe stir the bastard into moving?"

"*If* anyone's even in it," Kit said, again mumbling her words.

"Your coilgun is the only weapon we've got that'll reach it, unless I paint it." Roy shook his head.

He returned his focus to the IR scanners on his HUD. No readings for the quarry.

"Thermals aren't turning up shit."

No survivors, from their vantage point anyway. There was no telling how many personnel might still be alive inside the compound itself. But the vehicles…

Paired with Donnie's magnified optics, he and Roy confirmed that something very ugly had happened here. Well before their arrival.

Every vehicle not on its side or roof either spewed smoke from an engine compartment, solar panel, or was occupied by a bloodied corpse. Two instances, Donnie reported, where trucks' windshields were fragmented and sprayed red, but otherwise empty.

Kit, though not as capable as her teammates of enhanced optics, did note something very interesting. Enormous tracks in the sand-like dirt miring most of the sprawling compound. Not footprints, either, but the likes of which a snake would leave in its wake.

Except…colossal.

Some, nearly the width of an *Onslaught*.

This unsettled their already disturbed stomachs. But none of the pilots let it show in their voices.

"I hate to say it," Donnie pressed into the silence that had settled over their comms. "But if we can't confirm that their operation is *beyond salvage*, that second payment goes to the wind."

Roy hoarsely sighed.

"I'll scout," he volunteered.

"Love the spirit," Donnie said, and then his tongue clicked. His voice was firm, but not despotic. "But no. You will provide overwatch from this ledge, and keep an eye on that *Tarantula*."

He turned his *Adder*'s torso to face the *Kodiak*.

Roy mirrored the gesture.

"I won't bitch," he said, rather bluntly. "But would appreciate a reason."

"Kit and I will sweep the quarry," Donnie elaborated. "We're lighter on the feet, and I have a feeling the rest of the compound will be eaten up soon. Sooner if we tempt the sinkholes."

Roy nodded. "Good call."

"If it wasn't so much ground to cover," Donnie added, "and so many potential openings, I'd volunteer *just* Kit. But…"

"It is what it is," Roy said. "I'll cover you, and when Wyatt catches up, you'll have a *Raider* to boot."

"Good. Just tell him no LRMs. You, either. The smallest explosion could send Kit and I into the guts of Elnath."

"Copy. Ballistics and energy only."

"Watch the buildings, too," Kit chimed in, a bit worriedly. Justifiably. "A PPC could rupture a fuel depot or natural gas junction and gulp us in a white flash."

"Great point," Donnie said. "Feed that to Wyatt, will you?"

"No need, boss." The old man's raspy voice slid its way back onto their com-link. "But I agree. Nessa does, too."

"How's she holding up?" Roy asked, newfound relief entering his bloodstream.

"Get in on this," Wyatt muttered.

A second later, Nessa's voice graced their ears. They all envisioned exactly what was happening in the *Raider* cockpit. Nessa shadowed Wyatt, behind his seat, leaning over his shoulder so that her voice could be picked up by his helmet's integrated mic.

"I'm fine, everyone. Worst part of this was being under the Elnath sun for two minutes. Glad I ditched my vest."

"You seem like a chivalrous enough man, Wyatt Palmer," Roy said, all too sarcastically. At first. "So don't make me regret this decision."

"I'll restrain myself. Worst-case, she kicks my ass and takes the *Raider*."

A few snickers, including Nessa's own.

"Hell, I wouldn't mind stealing that *T*," she added. "Is it playing the staring game or just for show?"

"Undecided," Roy said. "Wyatt, does your TAC pick up anything?"

"Uh…" Wyatt flipped a switch, adjusted his optics, and focused on the *Tarantula*. Its gunmetal armor and exposed black joints emanated no iota of heat or electric signal. "Negative. It's either shut-down or empty."

"Yeah. Well, let's hope the latter."

"Okay, let's get this done," Donnie said. "Kit, take the lead. If I, or you, detect any instability under those light feet, we fall back to the inlet."

"Got it. Advancing."

Her *Shieldmaiden* proceeded, parallel to the long cliff edge, to a corner 120 meters away. Here, the quarry was at its shallowest, providing a natural ramp down into its pit. Ample for any number of heavy vehicles and equipment, including Mechs.

This was probably the most stable part of the entire quarry, so it didn't worry them the slightest during their descent. They continued at sixty-percent speed, not growing warier until they were feet-down in the actual quarry. Much of the ground had given way to a softer sand-like soil. This sediment was distinguishable from the solid ground in coloration, however subtle. The sand was browner than the paleness of the terrain surrounding them, including the harsh cliff faces.

Sporadically Kit and Donnie spun their torsos and pitched back to glance up at the opposing ledge. As if waving or saluting to their overwatch, the imposing outlines of the *Raider* and *Kodiak*.

Primarily, they focused on the Starchitect mining compound. The buildings were never taller than them, even before Elnath had decided to gobble the facility. Half the point of employing a Mech security detail was to have superior surveillance. The highest part of the surviving structures were nearly shoulder-height on the *Shieldmaiden*, just ten feet under Donnie's cockpit. These rooftops were not designed for personnel presence, nor were there an abundance of windows, both of which made scouting the property less perilous for the pilots.

It also let them keep occasionally glance at the distant *Tarantula*, even knowing that the others had a more vigilant eye on it.

"Nothing so far," Kit said, minding every entry-way she passed. Left and right.

"Likewise," Donnie contributed, double-checking the places she looked.

"No activity up here," Roy said. "Down there, or the *T.*"

Behind Wyatt, Nessa's brow furrowed. She had less a concept of etiquette compared to, say, Kit, which was why she startled Wyatt a little when she abruptly pointed at his canopy. She practically hung over his right shoulder, and for a moment Wyatt simply stared at her looming arm. Then he followed her finger, it quickly dawning on him that she had noticed something without the aid of his HUD. No magnified optics or thermal imaging.

Mere movement had caught her keen eye.

Wyatt idly recalled the famed battle stories about the Twin Dragons. In that instant he agreed to never second-guess, doubt, or underestimate the prowess of either Nessa or her brother.

He adjusted his aiming reticle, and zoomed out.

"I...*we*...are tracking movement at your two o'clock."

Roy's brow furrowed at Wyatt's declaration. He adjusted his optics northeast of Kit. She and Donnie had just emerged from a curving path between buildings, the one to their right partially engulfed in sand.

"There's nothing up there," Roy said, observing an expanse of terrain in the direction of the *Tarantula*, which remained inert. "Literally. No vehicles, tracks, or—"

Donnie was ready to agree with Roy, as he and Kit were looking in that direction after significantly slowing down. They were essentially in the open now, buildings to their left but nothing to their right. Ahead of them the path curved to the left, where more of the compound awaited them, albeit partially buried.

Then, undeniable movement.

A geyser of sediment misted the air forty meters in that direction.

As if water ejected from a whale's blowhole.

"The hell was that?" Kit asked.

"Gas pocket, maybe," Donnie shrugged. "Roy, remember what Kit said about the natural—"

Gunfire erupted to their immediate left. Bullets pattered the armor on their Mechs' legs, and both pilots pivoted to look down. Surprisingly enough, the security guards that had emerged from the building looked battered and dirty. Moreover, they now raised their Imperators up, before ditching the weapons altogether, and waving their arms.

"The shit?" Donnie muttered.

"I think…I think they want us to take them." Kit swallowed. "*Save* them."

"Psh. Fat chance. Unless they pick up those guns again, we leave them. Now push."

Kit sighed and stepped forward. The ground shook, and both pilots felt the tremor even up in their cockpits. Then the building at Donnie's five o'clock buckled, and crumbled to a new sinkhole. Smoke and debris sputtered into the air, washed down by a brief cyclone of sediment.

"Push, Kit!" Donnie snapped.

She advanced, giving Donnie room to space himself from the sinkhole and its pull. Simultaneously, the screams of men behind them could be heard, however faintly at first. Followed by gunfire, and when they turned there was no ignoring it anymore.

Serpentine creatures, the color of oxidized rust, with horn-like crests above their snouts, had emerged from the ground. They hissed and swatted their jaws at the two men, but only one of them had managed to retrieve his gun. He now fired and shouted, while the other man's head and torso vanished inside the second creature's mouth. It shook violently, pulled away, and guts splashed the ground. His legs wobbled, almost cartoonishly, before falling.

"Fuck me, we've got more of those alien snake-things down here," Donnie said, pivoting around to engage the creature from behind it.

"More like…wretched, goddamn carnivorous *worms*."

He didn't wholeheartedly agree with Kit's assessment, but wasn't going to complain for…reasons.

"Fine by me," he said, isolating his right Autocannon and disengaging burst-fire. "Anything to alienate them from my precious *Adder*."

"Whatever they are, can you kill 'em?" Wyatt asked. "The pilot back there was able to, with as little as a rifle. Though I suspect it was an unpleasantly close call."

"Copy, trying to avoid unnecessary casualties in the process."

Donnie shelled a single round at his target, and the 90mm projectile annihilated the latter half of the "worm" attacking the lone survivor. Blue blood hosed from the wound, streaking the ground. The man went to retreat back into the building, screaming as he went.

The Autocannon cycled, and Donnie's finger was ready to squeeze the solid red trigger. But Kit's rotary opened up, tracking the second worm as it slithered after the man. With a bead on her target, she cut the creature into pieces in barely a second's time. Not even its entire length had exited the soft ground.

"Good shooting," Donnie said, with relief.

"Want me to dismount, chase down the guard, and pull his heart out myself?" Kit asked with a bite.

"Fuck's sake, Kit."

"What?" She scoffed, chuckling sarcastically. "You *said*. Beyond salvage. That means, no survivors."

"Not…necessarily." Donnie flipped his visor up and kneaded his brow, then wiped sweat from it, and lowered the visor again. His eyes readjusted to the projected HUD on his canopy. "What's one guard to us, or

Ferrocore for that matter? The Mech threats are elimi-nated, nevermind that *T*. The compound is *sinking*. I think we've confirmed enough."

"Technically," Wyatt said, regrettably, "we're still missing two Mechs from the line-up. According to the contract."

"Probably swallowed by Elnath herself," Donnie shrugged. "Say, Roy?"

"I'm here, boss."

Donnie was shocked to hear him use that word, ever so casually, but not without conviction. He sup-posed that after everything that had happened on Elnath today, no man or woman in their presence was without the other's respect.

He chewed up his pause, spit it out, and finally answered.

"Record your feed. If—"

"Already on it," Wyatt interrupted.

"Great. Get wide shots, and close-ups. Don't stop recording 'til we're starbound."

"Gladly."

"If Ferrocore thinks we should do more for that second payment, we'll come back and blast it all to hell." Donnie clapped his hands, then snapped his fin-gers. "For now, we're shooting stars."

"Can't argue with that," Roy said.

"And the *Gunslinger*?" Wyatt asked.

"What about it?" Donnie sighed. During all of this, Kit was patrolling ahead, minding her footing. She remained suspicious of the open area of the quarry at her two o'clock. No more movement since then, and the building behind them had since vanished into the jaws of the planet.

"It went back to pick-up the other pilot."

Donnie shrugged. "I don't blame 'em. And neither should we, unless they open fire on us."

"A well-placed slug from just one of its Gauss rifles could devastate the *Shieldmaiden*."

Nessa's voice.

Inside the *Raider* cockpit, Wyatt sighed and gently pushed her away from his helmet. She scoffed and shrugged.

"I'm well aware," Donnie said. "Worst-case, if we even *sense* it looking at her, we'll cut its legs out. Hell, I'll green-light Kit to circle it and do the deed herself."

"All for it," Kit said, concern tickling her tone. "But I do agree with you, Donnie. Let 'em go. Unless."

"Unless, exactly. Okay, everyone. Wyatt?"

"Recording."

"Good. Kit? Come back around, take us outta this cesspool."

"Moving."

It wasn't until Donnie moved his *Adder* that another tremor shook the ground beneath them. Perhaps, though not immensely heavier than the *Shieldmaiden*, it was just enough tonnage to disturb whatever had been lying in wait.

The path between the Mud Wolves gaped via a jagged crater, Elnath's crust subject to the ophidian maggots infesting its bowels. The worm, or whatever word befit it most, was nearly four times the size of the "smaller" ones they had seen so far. It rose with an impish shriek, like a massive tapeworm with a rocky topside as if natural armor, and an exposed rust-orange belly. Its true size unknown, given that only the first few hundred feet had emerged, and from the crater slithered smaller ones, toward the Mechs.

Their horn-like crests sparked and both pilots experienced disruption in their systems. The colossal worm didn't have any crest, but its size and might alone were too imposing.

"Give that thing all you got, sans missiles," Roy ordered.

He and Wyatt targeted the massive worm, whose tail-end appeared eighty meters behind it, rising through the ground to spawn another sinkhole in the open.

"Fuck, this thing's huge!" Wyatt exclaimed.

"No wonder they had an *Onslaught* on their roster," Nessa, in the background on his comms. "They must've had *some* idea, no?"

"Either that or just paranoid," Wyatt said, and unleashed a pair of PPC jabs. One missed by a dozen meters, as the worm's body, though thirty feet across, was constantly squirming in the air. The other impacted but was completely dissipated by its armored topside.

"Focus!" Roy snapped. "Save the theories for when we're rich and drunk!"

Nobody contested that creed.

The smaller—it seemed a crime to attach that adjective to them—worms coiled around Donnie and Kit's Mechs. Directing his torso away from Kit, Donnie prepared to fire, but didn't know what.

"I need eyes on!" he shouted. "Roy, Wyatt—one of you. Assist. Where are these fuckers!?"

Suddenly one of the tapeworm-like creature slapped its underbelly onto his canopy, with a heavy and hollow *thump* that made his eardrums vibrate.

"Gotcha, bitch," Donnie growled.

He armed his SRMs, right thumb kneading the firing stud. Inset beneath the overhang of his nose-like cockpit, the missile module was clearly lined up with the bottom half of the worm on his canopy.

He fired.

The warheads, unlike LRMs, had no minimum arming distance, and exploded when they impacted the creature's underbelly. Only four did, the other two winded off before dropping to the ground. The small blasts collided and blew the worm in half, including its armored "scalp." As its gory-blue remains slid off his Mech, the other one slithered where he couldn't see.

"Kit, left arm!" Wyatt snapped. "Squirming onto your back!"

Kit spun her RAC, and the linked barrels of the rotary Autocannon caught an edge of the worm's "armor." It pulled the thing between the weapon and her shield-like forearm, crushing its belly to pulp. The tail-end flopped to the ground, but somehow the top half continued to slither over her shoulder.

The giant worm between them had begun to move *away*, for a reason none of them had the time or focus to notice. Except for Nessa, whose unmagnified view of the quarry allowed her certain liberties. She spotted a jab of PPC energy from the opposite end of the pit, and lined up the enemy *Tarantula*. It had stirred to life, strictly to engage the massive worm. Which was a huge task for one Mech, much less a Lightweight, but perhaps after witnessing the annihilation of their crew— and employers—the operator had amassed his or her courage.

Recklessness, whatever the word.

Nessa saw courage. And even though Mech pilots generally refused to call the operator of a *Tarantula* "pilot," or even "machinehead," she was ready to make an exception. Enemy or not.

Meanwhile, below, Kit gawked up at the alien worm attempting to crash through her canopy. Despite missing its bottom half, the ophidian jaws continued to drool and hiss, opening wide like a constrictor preparing to swallow its prey. Rows of small yet sharp, curved teeth screeched as they grinded against the ferroglass above her. She was literally staring into its pink gullet and didn't like it one bit.

Then the other worm appeared on her right arm. She glimpsed its horned head attempt to fit into the muzzle of her PPC barrel. She couldn't help but laugh as she triggered the weapon; her HUD might be disrupted from their EMP crests, but the crew's weapons still functioned properly.

Capacitors charged and then fired, obliterating the creature's head and ten feet of its body behind it. Crest and all.

Donnie was beginning to backpedal and grow tired of this enemy.

"Left arm…wait, right leg…no, shoulder!"

Roy wasn't helping, but Donnie didn't blame him. This particular worm was proving especially elusive, and annoying.

"Looks like it's making a move for your vents!" Roy said.

Kit and Wyatt remembered the sight of the smaller worms crawling forth from the enemy *Adder*'s shoulder vents. Donnie cringed, then bared his teeth before stuffing the mouthpiece in.

"Follow, Kit!" He mustered a hint of intelligibility. She heard, and complied, even with the halved worm still gnawing on her canopy.

With his own rarely obstructed by the slithering worm, Donnie had a clear enough line-of-sight to make it back to the quarry inlet. He noticed Roy's *Kodiak* leave its overwatch position to follow their progress, and didn't object.

"Everyone," Wyatt said, a new gravity to his voice. "Nessa brought it to my attention, but now it's clear as day. The big one—it's going after the *Tarantula*. Spidey started up just to engage the damn thing."

"We'll thank them later," Donnie said. "Roy, are you ready for some warranted FF?"

"Not really."

"Just pretend you hate how goddamn pretty I am."

"Pretend?"

Donnie smirked. He wasn't a huge fan of *ordering* another pilot to commit friendly-fire, but given the circumstances he saw no other option. With armor integrity above 80%, some Laser burns wouldn't hurt him, or his feelings. Especially from a talented pilot like *the* Roy Alcott. He would almost prefer Kit's RAC to do the job, but didn't want to risk catching a bullet to his vents, and besides, she was dealing with her own issues.

Below the tenacious worm latched onto her canopy, Kit felt something tickle her neck. She shrugged repeatedly, and then felt a light pain. Seconds later she realized it was glass dust, sprinkling down and catching the collar of her jumpsuit.

"Fuck's sake, the thing's actually puncturing my canopy," she growled.

"Let me blast it to shit," Roy offered.

"I don't know, man, I'm not as nuts as Donnie is."

"I'll use my Lasers on him, I'll use my MG on you. Nessa can vouch for my aim."

Kit mumbled something incoherent. More glass dust sprinkled her shoulders, and a foul stench seeped into her cockpit.

"I'll stall, make myself dizzy," Donnie said, as he reached the inlet ramp and throttled up it.

"Copy. Kit, full stop. Trust me."

Donnie branched to the left, reaching the crest of the ramp and running his Mech in a tight circle. Simultaneously, he rotated his torso back and forth, as jerkily as he could. If he was unable to sling the worm off his *Adder*, he would at least keep it from stuffing itself into his vents.

In the meantime, Kit finally gave in and halted her *Shieldmaiden*. Blue gore dripped from its left arm, and a snail-trail of it had snaked around the Mech's shoulder, and up the back of its cockpit-head. But the wounded worm was about to receive its final injury—

Roy's *Kodiak* paused at the top of the inlet, bowed his torso twelve degrees, and meticulously fired his chin-mounted machineguns. The two barrels flashed and a staccato stream of .50-caliber rounds hit their mark. One rang off the *Shieldmaiden*'s shoulder armor, and another grazed her canopy, but it would take more than that to penetrate the ferroglass. Less, though, given its already compromised integrity.

Kit winced but watched with heightening relief as the worm was blasted away. Chunks of orange flesh and blue innards flopped down her canopy, a fragment or two of its brown crest pattering the ferroglass.

"All clear," Roy said, but didn't have time to gloat. He spun around to focus on Donnie, but was relieved when he saw the worm slithering on the ground, attempting to burrow into the steppe.

The *Adder*'s pronged right foot stamped its tail-end, pancaking crest and flesh into the terrain. The rest of it broke free and began to burrow, but Donnie muttered "no, you don't" before two green Lasers minced it into pieces just behind its head. The organism stopped moving altogether.

Donnie turned to face Roy's *Kodiak.*

"Hold your fire, buddy."

Roy laughed boisterously. He was allowed a breath of victory and reprieve.

"Oh, boy." He finally sighed. "That was…unnecessarily intense."

"You're telling me," Kit sighed. "Appreciate it, though. *I* might have to buy us a drink, now."

"Let's wait to hold hands, folks," Wyatt said. "We've still got a problem that's about ninety meters long and ten wide. Suggestions? The *T* seems overwhelmed."

The *Tarantula* appeared to be holding its ground relatively well, all things considered. Its maneuverability was proving superior at the helm of its competent pilot, taking advantage of the larger worm's lesser mobility. Still, the thing was agiler than its mass would suggest.

"Fuck suggestions," Kit said, and immediately accelerated toward that end of the quarry, once topside. She stayed close to the cliff edge, light on her feet and feeling a renewal of energy.

"Kit, goddammit," Donnie muttered.

"Sorry, boss, but I agree. Give the *T* some credit, and let's help the poor sumbitch if we can."

Donnie sighed, and began to follow her, issuing the order.

"Wyatt, Roy—on my six."

He gathered his own wits, courage, and didn't ignore the thrill of battle, or the merit that the *Tarantula* operator deserved. For now.

"But don't wait to engage it," he added.

They didn't need to be told twice.

9

At last a faction again, or as close to one given Nessa's desertion of her *Lancer*, the combined crews moved in a strafing column toward the far end of Cauldron Quarry. Its largest tenant, a massive subterranean worm captured on Wyatt's video feed, was enduring attacks now from not only one war machine, but five. At ground-level, beneath its snaky mass, the nimble *Tarantula* likely neared automatic-shutdown levels of heat from salvos of combined armaments. These included a Middleweight-caliber PPC, four 20mm Autocannon barrels, four medium-bore Lasers, and two machineguns.

The closer they got, there wasn't a pilot among them—Donnie included—that would turn down a drink with that pilot.

Man or woman.

The salvos from the Mud Wolves—and Roy—were sufficed to irritate the massive worm enough to take its attention off the skittering *Tarantula*. Its enormous tail lifted through the ground, annihilating nearly half of the remaining compound buildings in the process, and swung toward the side of the quarry that their Mechs flanked.

Straggling once more, the slowest of the lot, Wyatt's *Raider* was the only one vulnerable. He jerked back on his throttle at the last second, before the blunt tail-end of the worm crashed into the cliff ledge a mere twenty feet away.

The Mech lumbered to a stop in time, navigated away from the ledge, but still rotated its torso to fire at the worm's upper half. Both PPCs missed wide, but he managed to drag his Lasers down its side, drawing blood that cauterized nanoseconds later. Already scorched and bleeding from various other wounds, the worm seemed to finally admit defeat and retreat.

"I think it's tallying the L," Donnie said, with grave relief.

"A shame, I really wanted to see its guts on the ground," Kit practically snarled. She had damn near reached the opposite end of the quarry, where the *Tarantula* now strode toward.

"He needs to watch out for its ass-end," Wyatt muttered, as he witnessed the worm's latter half trough through the ground, toward the *Tarantula*. It was merely in tandem with its withdrawing maneuver, however, not an attack.

Donnie fired his shoulder-mounted coilguns again for the hell of it, reticle lined up with the creature's backside. The slugs cut the air and reached their target, one lodging into the crest and another shattering a chunk of it. The worm shrieked out before plunging its tapered skull into the bulk of the Starchitect compound, caving it into the bowels of Elnath.

What remained of the mining facility seemed to cave inward in a final display of ruination.

Geysers of sand-like sediment sprayed the air, an occasional burp of fire erupted, and more smoke billowed into the atmosphere.

"You get all that?" Donnie asked.

"If you say *corrupted file*, or, uh, *not recording*..." Roy let heavy, haggard breaths carry over the com-link. "Oh, I'm gonna go berserk."

Wyatt laughed a bit raucously.

"Fellas, fellas. Ladies, too, uh, try to relax. I've got forty terabytes available, and this has all put me at three. I think we're good."

Relieved exhalations across the channel.

Then, it sputtered with new life.

"Hello? Anyone there?"

For an enemy Mech to piggyback another crew's com-link was a kind of sorcery that only skilled technicians could pull off. This *Tarantula* pilot was proving more and more worth his salt.

"Anyone, please? Don't fire. I appreciate the help, but, uh..."

The voice trailed off. It was masculine, but a little tinny. Young. If the tone matched their presumed age range of the pilot, the crew would be all the more impressed.

"You're cornered, we see," Donnie said, noticing that the quadrupedal Mech was essentially trapped against the base of one cliff face, eighty percent of the quarry now an enormous chasm.

"I don't think you're making it to the inlet," Kit said, shaking her head.

"Any ideas?" he asked.

"How'd you get on this channel, first," Roy asked, one eyebrow raised.

"Oh, uh, a little techie trick I learned on Phecda."

Donnie was colored impressed. A Fleet-protected planet in the Ursa system, Phecda was like an apprenticeship for a lot of the Mech techs that now made a living on Alcor.

"What's your name, bud?" Wyatt asked.

"Webber." He cleared his throat. "Cyril Webber. Starchitect employed me, I'm part of a dyad. Have you seen an *Adder* up there? Uh, the other one."

"Sister?" Nessa asked, leaning forward again.

"Christ, no. Wife."

"Good for you, Cyril," Kit smirked. "She's a tough broad. The, uh, *Gunslinger* picked her up about thirty minutes ago."

Wyatt's *Raider* pivoted around.

"I got eyes on," he said. "But TAC's out of range. They're moving, though."

"Thank you, thank you." Cyril sounded like a buoy floating in waves of relief. It was a bit short-lived, though. "So, um…care to maybe spare some ideas on how to get me outta here? We'll tell Starchitect to eat shit and buy ourselves a whole night at the pub."

"Can't object to that, Webber," Roy said. "That some, uh, bad joke or something, by the way? Putting you in a *Tarantula*, of all things?"

"You mean like a woman in a *Shieldmaiden*?"

"Easy, there," Kit said, albeit smiling to herself.

"It's actually a long story," Cyril chuckled awkwardly. "I'm as talkative as I am generous. About those drinks, guys…"

"You have any fear of heights, kid?" Wyatt asked.

"Um…not really. Why?"

"How many times have you ever ejected?"

"Oh, uh, I don't know. Ten, twelve."

Wyatt sighed, and exchanged head-shaking looks with Nessa before replying.

"ITF, Cyril. Not simulation."

"Shit, well, never."

"First time for everything," Kit said. Her *Shieldmaiden* turned toward Donnie. "Wanna take this one, boss? Apart from me, your *Adder* can get the lowest, and has the best off-center balance. My cockpit's too cramped, and my canopy's punctured."

Donnie Prescott took a long, deep breath, and let his dramatic expression carry over their frequency.

"Yeah, I suppose you're right. Cyril, was it?"

"I'm here."

"No, you're not. I want you in the air, in twenty seconds. Unless you wanna wait for those *alien worms* to come back for seconds."

The pilot didn't argue, or stall.

Donnie performing this wouldn't be the first time, which gave his mind some space to roam during the maneuver. He couldn't help but wonder, would Kit try to be a do-gooder and insist that Cyril here get a chunk of their Ferrocore reward?

Assuming they were paid in full, Donnie would ease his heart and conscience by volunteering a little donation to husband and wife. In honor of battlefield sportsmanship, tenacity against inhuman odds, and teamwork despite being on opposite sides of greedy employers.

If anything, Donnie would *pay* to never do work on Elnath ever again.

Warrior First

"The biggest reward for a thing well done is to have done it."

Voltaire

1

Great pines shuddered and snow from last week's blizzard burst into white dust when the missiles left their pods. The fauna inhabiting the copse could count their blessings as the *Kodiak* strode past it. Three-toed feet supporting seventy tons sunk through six inches of snow like it was melted butter, leaving muddy prints in the soil with each step. Ninety meters away, a white *Shieldmaiden* slalomed as if it could evade lock-on.

The *Kodiak* pilot tracked its target and fired an Autocannon at its legs. Agile and narrow, hitting this part of a moving Middleweight was only reserved for the most talented pilots. The first two-round burst missed, blowing explosive divots of snow and soil four to six meters from its feet.

A follow-up burst caught it below the hip, and the already injured *Shieldmaiden* staggered from the blow. Fragmented ferrosteel littered the surrounding terrain, carving into snow-slathered knolls.

Aric Vallon was getting annoyed.

He had muted his incoming-missile alarm, but couldn't ignore the red lights bathing his cockpit. The flurry of twelve LRMs volleyed his Mech from above. The last thing he saw before flame enveloped his canopy was just how close he had gotten to the factory's maintenance building.

Fifty meters.

So fucking close.

Four missiles detonated on the ground around him, but the other eight swathed the *Shieldmaiden*'s torso in coalescing explosions. The Middleweight rocked violently and his helmet's chinstrap snapped. Better than his neck, he figured.

Aric's left hand had slipped from the throttle during the salvo, despite the textured glove. His right hand kept the Mech's torso on a constant swivel, to ensure an even distribution of damage, in hopes of avoiding a concentration of armor loss.

He didn't have a lot of it to begin with, and had not been expecting an enemy *Kodiak* of all things.

According to his employer's contract, the weapons facility he was sent to sabotage would have no more than one Lightweight and one Middleweight as mechanized security. The exact models hadn't been specified, but already Aric tallied two separate victories.

He'd only been on Alzirr for three hours.

The first sixty-some minutes were spent scouting the 44-acre property from outside its perimeter. He managed to penetrate the inferior barrier with ease, and

199

annihilate the factory's central structures and ammunition depot within half an hour. During that time, as flames licked the evening sky and black smoke crept toward approaching thunderheads, he had only been tickled by a pair of *Cicadas*. The Lightweight Mechs darted around the property, occasionally tagging him with their Lasers.

A minor nuisance at best.

One in which Aric managed to halve by decommissioning a *Cicada* that dared cross his path. In an attempt to intervene him and sandwich his *Shieldmaiden* in a crossfire with the other *Cicada*, Aric made sure the pilot learned his lesson. He punched a small salvo of SRMs center-mass, and followed with a PPC blast that ignited a heatsink. The coolant explosion separated the *Cicada*'s gaunt right leg from its torso, and the twenty-foot Mech toppled.

Since then, Aric was down to two.

Although, if the contract had been accurate—when was it, ever?—he'd only be left with the surviving Lightweight.

As it turned out, there were no Middleweights in the factory's security detail. Just two *Cicadas* and…

"This fucking *Kodiak*," Aric muttered, as the flames cleared and his splintered rear camera gave him a glimpse of the enemy Mech.

Seventy meters away.

But, to his surprise, not closing.

It took a few avian-legged strides from the nearby copse at its back, stabbed at his *Shieldmaiden* with a pair of searing red Lasers, but otherwise didn't advance.

To his knowledge, there was a merc camp twenty klicks southeast of here. His LZ had been in the opposite direction, where his *Sabot* touched-down near the delta of an otherwise arid canyon. It was possible that the *Kodiak* had been employed by the factory to perform outer-perimeter patrols at certain hours of the day.

"How lucky can I be?" Aric thought out loud, a bite of sarcasm before he heard a sizzling pop. Loud enough to be a thunderclap, but the colossal clouds overhead were not alight just yet.

Another violent *pop* and his beloved Mech's left thigh fell into its shin. The knee actuator was gone. His cockpit canted to the left, and a harsh "fuck" snapped through his teeth.

Alarms flashed again.

If Aric made it out of this, he wondered if he would ever perceive a color that wasn't red.

The flight of LRMs from the enemy *Kodiak* were in the air. ETA—twelve seconds.

"Farewell, my love," Aric said, and put the *Shieldmaiden* into a crouch. This kept it from toppling altogether, though the groaning of metal was a harbinger of this unavoidable result. He proceeded to flip a myriad of switches and jab an array of keys on a pad to the left of his joystick—all in a specific order.

One error would nullify the process and require starting over. An option he didn't have.

Succeeding in nine seconds, the Mech's containment coils were disabled. On the eve of the tenth second, Aric put all his might into pulling up on the ejection handle.

His canopy detached, and the seat he was harnessed to propelled itself out of the exploding Mech, at a canted angle. The white-hot flash violated his clamped eyelids and a heat wave beneath his seat threatened to set his boots on fire.

A deafening sound raped his senses.

He could feel his hair follicles shudder, his very marrow vibrate.

In his nine years as a pilot, Alaric Vallon had never been this close to a fusion blast. He had also never had to scuttle his own Mech, and after half a decade in the *Shieldmaiden*, his heart broke for her.

Unprecedented nausea and a tickle of fear that he would die a coward fleeing his machine—

Aric lost consciousness in the air.

2

Shockwave-propelled debris wasn't a thing with a fusion blast. The Mech was vaporized, leaving only a crater and clumps of metal where its feet had been. The explosion itself, however, a mere thirty meters from the maintenance building, had an effect on the structure.

The anterior façade rattled, windows shattered, and doors erupted inward.

Anti-Mech personnel wielding handheld SRM launchers had been called to repel the interloper. Reports were coming in over the PA about support from the neighboring merc camp, and a *Kodiak* distinguished as a "friendly." Their target was a white *Shieldmaiden.*

The personnel amassed only to witness a blinding white flash through the windows. It was their last sight, and 2.7 seconds later they weren't on this plane.

Aric's strategy had been achieved.

He was fortunate enough to bear witness after the fact. Overlapping voices shouting and cursing, orders being barked and confirmed, riled him from the void. He sat up with a jerk, and soreness stretched through his limbs, but found favor in his neck.

Fearing he had torn a ligament or suffered a spinal injury, Aric couldn't resist screaming through his teeth as he stood.

There was a wobble before he found his equilibrium. Or a vestige of it, anyway.

Snow crunched under his boots, their soles partially melted. Steam rose up from the mud, and he plodded away from the seat his harness had torn from. Aric counted a plethora of blessings before falling to his knees. The coolness of the snow on his jumpsuit was a relief.

The paranoia of being burned, or melted, alive was now behind him. His vision corrected just in time for his ears to pick up an odd hiss. Then he looked over his shoulder and saw a terrible red Laser vanish from thin air, not ten meters behind him.

Eighty away, the menacing *Kodiak* stood.

He was only lucky that he had landed so close to the factory building that the Mech had been charged with protecting. Its pilot couldn't risk a direct hit, not if he or she had any semblance of ethos.

Aric's life banked on it, but he wasn't the most optimistic when it came to pilots-for-hire.

Even as one himself.

He got up, and stumbled forward with a new lease on life, as the *Kodiak* unleashed another jab with its large-bore Laser. The perfect red beam of concentrated heat zapped the snowy earth less than twenty feet behind him. Water, once snow, splashed his back as he lost his balance over a threshold. Formerly a heavy metallic door this side of the maintenance building, his immolated *Shieldmaiden* had turned it into an empty frame.

"Thanks, love," he muttered as he crawled to his hands and knees. Then, to his feet again, bracing himself against a concrete wall.

Aric set his eyes on the charred bodies of various armed personnel down a corridor to his right. Some of them had been spared from the fusion heat, and died of puncture wounds, according to a spray of jagged debris. Not from the Mech, but the windows and wall itself.

He shook his head.

A hell of a way to go, one he didn't necessarily wish for, but upon seeing SRM launchers in some of their hands, he accepted it.

Consequences of battle.

Aric searched their corpses for a usable weapon. A few of the men carried sidearms, but their holsters were either melted or the pistols themselves inoperable. One he managed to shuck free, but blood from its dead owner had clogged the slide latch.

As he cursed under his breath and tried clearing the jam, an eruption of voices stole his attention. A corridor perpendicular to the one he currently occupied.

He looked up. The intersection was seven or eight feet away. How close the voices sounded, and the rush of boots on pavement, made him drop the weapon. He backpedaled over the bodies, nearly tripping on one, and finally rallied the wherewithal to be of use to himself. Not just a stumbling, breathless victim of circumstance.

Aric reminded himself of…

Everything he had ever been, become, and was capable of doing.

He moved down the opposite corridor, just in time to remember the voices he heard before he pulled himself out of unconsciousness. Whoever was after him—the factory's security team, likely ex-infantry turned mercs, too—were split into groups.

The maintenance building had not been one of his contract's targets. Spared, it was now his new battlefield. Not one he was as used to as the cockpit of a

Mech, but something he could work with. Better than an open warehouse or transferring to one piece of cover to another in a field.

A network of narrow corridors, server rooms, storage closets, and the like.

He avoided heading down the nearing corridor, but would have to cross it to reach the staircase on the other side. He did so with little contemplation, knowing that every second mattered.

Several men shouted, and bullets zipped through the air behind him. Small chunks of concrete wall sprayed into the compact stairwell. Aric rebounded off a wall, steadied the breath in his throat, and then bounded up the next squat flight of steps. His right shoulder bumped into a fire extinguisher, and he cursed without moving his lips.

A wry smirk appeared on his face as his eyes set upon the archaic tool left of the extinguisher.

Tactical glove still on his left hand, but his right bare as it would to maneuver a joystick, he quietly lifted the fire axe from its hooks. The long, slightly curved composite handle felt at home in his clutches. The blade head, wedged to a fine point that shimmered briefly under an LED fixture, made his smirk fade.

Into a grim expression of determination.

Aric retreated behind the short wall left of the stairwell. He waited, bare hand beneath the blade head; gloved hand low, toward the butt.

Booted footfalls ascended the steps.

Rounded the first flight.

A fluted barrel belonging to an Imperator protruded from the stairwell. About waist-height. Aric sidled and swung. The axe blade caught a merc's temple and drove his head into the wall. Steel staved skull and a millimeter of blade lodged in the concrete, blood and brain matter slopping off it.

The mercs behind Aric's victim gasped and staggered back.

Then one pushed forward, shouting.

Aric wrenched the axe free and ducked, a blink of an eye before gunfire shredded the space where he'd just been standing. He rolled forward and his boots kicked off a wall to slide him out of the corridor and into a door. It burst in, bruising his shoulder but better than being chewed up by bullets.

A janitor looked at him with a dropped jaw.

Aric rose a gloved finger to his lips, and then waved at the older man with his other hand. The axe made a sound on the floor when his boots touched it and, still on his side, he spun to reach for it. When he glanced back into the room, he saw the janitor hoist himself through a window and begin clambering down the fire escape outside.

"Good man," Aric muttered.

He heard an Imperator open up and hammer the floor behind him. Bullets volleyed the metal door he had just opened, more zipping into the room he occupied. Crawling, axe in both hands as if a rifle, Aric put some distance between himself and the open doorway.

That he wasn't returning fire was their way of knowing that he was unarmed. The axe certainly confirmed it.

Still, the men camped outside the door, on either side of it.

One of them threw his voice.

"Pilot! Surrender now and we'll chalk up what you just did as panic."

The merc sounded gruff, relatively heavyset, and probably a massive pain in the ass at your local pub. Aric listened in one ear, but was focusing on crawling between desks, toward another door on the far side of the room.

"Logical," the merc added, snidely. "Considering your situation."

"*My* situation?" Aric laughed. A classical "ha!" following like a bite from a terrier. "*You* should *envy* my situation!"

"Are you mad? Machineheads aren't known for their soundness of mind. But open your eyes. You're outnumbered, outgunned, and someplace you don't know as well as we do."

Aric shook his head, grinning.

He had reached the door, which, if he was right, connected this room to the adjacent one. Worst-case, it was a closet. Then, his enemies might be right.

"Au contraire," he said, and the ensuing silence was punctuation enough.

Aric, on his back, retracted his legs before kicking them out at full force. The door, wood not metal like the others, buckled. A lock blew out and the door wobbled free of the jamb. Men outside the room shouted and poured in. Aric sprang to his feet but ducked as he rushed into the neighboring room, bullets battering the doorway he used.

Not a closet.

The storage room was, however, like an elaborate closet about twenty by twenty feet. Packed with floor to ceiling shelving and various items on them. From cleaning products to tools and spare server parts.

Aric kept low as he rat-in-a-maze navigated the room.

Bullets chased him.

They shredded everything around him, and part of the experienced pilot knew his luck had to be running thin. Still, he managed to reach the "exit" miraculously intact, and burst through it with relative ease.

Most of the mercs pursuing him were in the room he first entered, or making their way into the adjacent one. Two stragglers in the corridor, peering through the door, spotted him down the corridor.

They shouted and signaled.

Aric scrambled in the opposite direction. He managed to reach the nearest corner before gunfire erupted twenty meters behind him. He bumped into a pair of maintenance workers, their jumpsuits mottled with grease and their faces stained with fear. One was in his twenties, the other twice that, but they both wore an air of harmlessness.

Bystanders merely trying to do their lowly jobs.

Aric put a finger to his mouth, recalling how well it went last time.

The storm of voices over paused gunfire behind him made Aric glance over his shoulder.

Then a slamming door in front of him. When he looked, the younger worker had retreated into an equipment closet. The older one struggled with the doorknob, but it wasn't budging.

Aric started to move past him.

The middle-aged man began shouting at the top of his lungs, his voice wavering. Most of his words didn't count as words, but Aric did catch "here, over here" several times.

"Fuck's sake," Aric grumbled, and advanced down the hall.

He tried the next nearest door but it wouldn't budge. Then another, twenty feet down. Locked. He cursed under his breath and moved to the next. Bullets cut the air around him. A pain erupted in his leg. He dove at a space in the concrete wall at shoulder-height. A window pane shattered in his wake and he tumbled into the room behind it. He landed on a desk, rolled off it, papers fluttering around him.

When Alaric got to his feet, more or less, he noticed the axe had fallen from his hands. He used his gloved one to pull a two-inch shard of glass from his right tricep, grimacing and suppressing a sound. Blood spilt onto the floor. A sweaty, haggard breath stumbled out of his mouth as he dropped the glass.

It occurred to him that he was in an archives room. Where paper documents were being scanned into electronic databases. These were nonexistent in Fleet-funded facilities, but common elsewhere.

Aric recalled his contract. The Fleet encoding. He thought it was just a precaution. Now he wondered if this place was really manufacturing weapons for some kind of terrorist maneuver against Ursa. A radical and foolhardy plan, but not unheard of.

"There, there, in there!"

That damn worker was still spouting off.

Aric sighed and looked around. The lights were off. At least the room was empty. But the only door in or out was farther down the corridor, too close to the end where his enemies amassed.

He moved toward the window he had just crashed through, and kicked away pieces of glass from the floor below it. He squatted and turned, flattening himself against the concrete wall, his disheveled hair hardly two inches from the sill.

"On me, on me, prepare to open fire," one of the mercs ordered. Aric recognized the gruff voice.

Booted footfalls followed. Then stopped.

"Steady," another voice announced, farther away. He turned his head and spotted a shadow shift twenty feet down the wall. Paired with an opening door.

They were breaching the room; Aric pictured a stout column of three or four mercs moving through the doorway down the corridor. He glimpsed the first man enter, sweeping a Reaper before him. Aric would've donated a quarter of his contract if it guaranteed he never had to encounter a Reaper on-foot. Much less in the confines of a room he wasn't familiar with. The drum-fed assault shotgun was anyone's worst nightmare in close quarters.

Above and behind him, Imperator barrels protruded. Then boots and legs.

The rest of the mercenary group were entering the room through the shattered window.

Aric gulped and prepared a last-ditch effort.

Bodies alighted to his left and right. He shimmied inches at a time to ensure he wasn't stepped on, but half of it was sheer luck.

The man with the shotgun was followed by an SMG-wielding merc with a flashlight attached where a bayonet should be. The beam cut through the room. Behind him, another flashlight-mounted SMG. No fourth man. The rest of the mercs were either still in the corridor or had entered the room—

Either side of Aric, some in front.

They had not detected him yet.

Then someone's leg brushed him and Aric's heart sank. The man flinched, turned, and his eyes widened as he gawked down at the fugitive pilot.

Before his voice could catch up, the merc was shoved backwards. Aric had put eighty percent of his weight into the shoulder-check. He rebounded off the surprised merc, who stumbled into his comrades, and vaulted through the empty window frame.

Overlapping shouts came after him.

Followed by bullets.

There was a crossfire of panic, as two mercs were still in the corridor when Aric reentered it. He bumped into them; in fact, they kept him from crashing to the floor. Men inside the room realized they had been bested now fired their weapons angrily in his direction.

Aric was a few paces down the corridor when he turned and saw the two dumbstruck mercs take a dozen rounds center-mass. He almost felt bad for the men, clearly led by an incompetent soldier.

Axe in tow, Aric continued. He turned a corner and nearly busted his lip on a pair of double-doors. They were locked. The sound of chains rattled on the other side. He cursed under his breath and tried again.

Nothing.

"Fuck," gnashed through his teeth.

A small victory followed by a mortifying failure. Was this the end of the road for Alaric Vallon?

3

Surrender became an itch he refused to scratch. As voices and profanity assembled around the corner and down the corridor from him, he realized that only two options were available. A white flag, or suicide. In a manner of speaking, both went hand-in-hand.

Aric looked around.

He only had about six feet to maneuver. He truly had turned the corner too fast and nearly head-butted the doors in the process. It was a terrible corridor design, and the placement of the doors made him want to hunt down the architect himself.

An electrician's crawlspace.

By his left boot. He kicked it, and the grate rattled. Another kick that left his toes aching, and it came off. The sound was jarring. Voices from his enemies paused to listen.

Aric knelt, bowed his head, and stuck it into the small opening. It was dark and narrow.

As a seasoned Mech pilot, claustrophobia wasn't in his lexicon. Beyond that, he feared he might get stuck. He was neither robust nor gaunt, but an athletic median. It seemed feasible.

Footfalls echoed down the corridor behind him.

"Now or never," he sighed, and raised to a knee. He gathered the axe in his hands, cranked it back, shuffled closer to the corner, and then swung it as hard as he could. He loosed the handle from his grip at the last second. The axe swirled down the corridor. The composite handle struck someone's leg, causing a minor pain. The blade caught another merc's shin and lodged into the bone. He cried out and staggered, toppling another.

Those behind them rushed forward, vaulting the wounded men. Turning the corner, they saw a dead-end and a pair of doors that didn't budge. It wasn't until their comrades joined them that their boots nudged a dislodged grate on the floor, and the crawlspace drew their attention.

Aric crawled into the adjacent corridor, stretching as he stood up, in time to hear a burst of profanity on the other side of the chained double-doors.

An iota of pride made him smirk.

Then the PA system crackled to life.

"Intruder is in the southeast wing, maintenance building B."

Whoever made the announcement wasn't the gruff merc he conversed with earlier. This person was less bitter, but somehow more resolute.

And then came the cherry on top, for Aric.

"Intruder has destroyed central processing and both ammo depots," the announcement continued. There, he detected—a *hint* of bitterness. "He is armed and dangerous. Detain alive, if possible."

Aric set his back against the flat concrete wall, and gathered his breath. A rush of vitality seeped into his system. Something he wasn't expecting.

A confirmation of his accomplishments.

Aric's contract had been executed without a fault. The destruction of his Mech, and now his evasion, were risks every pilot faced in any combat situation. That he didn't die with the *Shieldmaiden* simply complicated his situation.

It didn't mar his achievement.

Much to his surprise, though, Aric didn't have a shoot-on-sight order on his head. He suspected it might be inevitable, though.

The now-too-familiar din of boots and gear rustling, paired with hushed voices, caught his ear. He turned his head and inched toward the end of the corridor he occupied. It divided into a T-intersection, two opposing routes. He couldn't track from which direction the clamor was coming from.

So he had to take a chance.

One among many.

A thought occurred to him. He turned, and rushed back toward the chained double-doors. The dead-end he had initially fled from. As he neared it, the front half of a merc emerged from the crawlspace. He kicked the man in the face, and there was a sickening *crunch*. He stooped, wrenched the man's weapon from his clutches, dropped to a knee, and thrusted the SMG into the crawlspace.

"Back up, back up, back—"

He suppressed the voices by squeezing the trigger. Gunfire rattled through the narrow crawlspace, some ricocheting off surfaces and armored helmets, but most lodging in vests and flesh.

The magazine went dry and he ejected it, then dragged the first merc's body into the corridor. He turned him over, noticed where his neck had swollen from a broken vertebra, and policed his pouches for additional ammunition.

Two mags for the SMG, one for a pistol, and the sidearm itself. He unholstered it, stuffed its bulk into a pocket on his jumpsuit, and two-handed the SMG.

An eruption of anger from the other side of the double-doors. A particular voice filtered through the crawlspace.

"Brains over brawn, sorry, bud," Aric shrugged.

He turned and rushed back toward the intersecting corridors. He peered around a corner and spotted a different cluster of mercs advancing, twenty meters down. Two up front pointed and shouted.

Arcis' brow furrowed and his jaw clenched.

He spun into the open, but dropped to a knee and fired. The Cutter SMG sprayed, 8.5mm rounds rattling down the corridor. One merc went down, another dropped to match his height, proving competence for once. Bullets hosed out at him, and Aric rolled back.

"Get him back, take him back!"

"Push!"

"No, hold, goddammit!"

Aric listened. He lifted the Cutter and inspected the magazine. Portholes in the side revealed it was at half-capacity. He breathed through funneled lips, and rose to his feet, back still to the wall.

He stared down the opposite corridor.

Getting shot in the back wasn't on his to-do list, but he saw no other route.

Aric ran.

His right shoulder struck the opposite wall and he bounced off it, pain resounding in his tricep where glass had been fifteen minutes ago.

Voices and gunfire pursued him.

He flinched as any human would, and his breathing became choppy. He bounded down the corridor, in a building he realized was, by now, largely evacuated. It had been converted into a hunting ground with one prey in mind.

Aric Vallon.

They of course didn't know his name. And they wouldn't, unless he saw fit that they did. Half the reason for immolating the *Shieldmaiden* was surrendering its identity and the contract he'd accepted to the void. If this place really was under the operation of a terrorist cell, he'd be damned if they knew any more about him that he allowed.

He wasn't at *their* mercy.

It was the other way around, and he would fight tooth and nail to make sure it stayed that way.

Aric cut right, raised his boot, and kicked open a door. It swung inward, clashed against a wall, and a catacomb of towering black servers surrounded him. A myriad of lights blinked at him, as if endless eyes studying his movements. Trying to deduce the code of conduct he operated on.

No, Aric convinced himself—

They were just lights.

This was a server room. There were two to three in each maintenance building. He looked around, and immediately felt the heat wafting off of them. A bevy of heatsinks were integrated into the floor around them, and his semi-melted boot treads caught on one. He tripped and bumped into another column of servers. A switch flipped, a wire detached.

Alarms rang, briefly scrambling his brains.

Then they shut off, and only a muted light flashed, washing the dark room in a staccato white glow.

"You want alarms?" Aric muttered.

He backed up, retracing his steps. The door was behind him, but so was the approaching clamor of footsteps and angry voices.

Aric recalled the *Cicada* and *Kodiak*.

Moreover, the expanse of terrain surrounding this facility. He was half a day's trek, on foot, to his D-class freighter. He hated to even entertain the thought, but suspected that the *Sabot* was currently being raided by enemy forces, either seized for parts or possibly even scuttled.

Aric wasn't leaving this rock.

He acknowledged this much.

Sure, Alzirr was a big place. But, circumstances considered, so was this property. Forty-four acres of personnel that wanted him dead, and an adamant *Kodiak* that his employer hadn't accounted for, on his ass.

Aric's heels paused at the threshold.

He extended the Cutter in front of him, both hands wielding it, and squeezed the trigger. Squinting as the muzzle flash lit up the server room, bullets hosing out at 1,100 rounds-per-minute.

The mag went dry and Aric loaded his last, plucked from his left pocket. He racked the firing lever with a snap, spat out another ten rounds, then movement caught his right eye.

He left the server room in a storm of blaring alarms, hissing steam, sparking heatsinks, and—

An explosion rocked the corridor.

A belch of flame from the doorway behind him. Aric staggered toward the end of the corridor, bounced off a locked door, and into another. This one budged, despite an engaged deadbolt. He backed up from it, raised his leg, and kicked as high as his foot could go. The bolt rattled but the door stayed.

Aric, heaving rugged breaths, shouldered the Cutter and drove the bayonet into a half-inch gap between door and jamb. The blade caught the bolt, screws popped from a wall mount, and finally the door opened. He lowered his shoulder and charged into the room.

"Everybody get down, down, *down*!" Aric shouted, the instant he laid eyes on personnel.

Men and women alike in uniform jumpsuits flinched, a few screamed on impulse, and they dropped. Some crouched, others went flat to the floor, prone, hands over their heads.

Aric walked the ten-by-twenty-meter room, gaze scanning the tables. He began to ask the key words—

What is this place?

But it quickly occurred to him.

Weapons and munitions either deemed defective or recalled, to be disassembled for parts.

"Everyone, move into the corridor!" he shouted, waving the Cutter.

Nobody budged.

"Fucking *move!*" He roared, and fired a two-round burst into the ceiling.

Scattered screams and whimpers. The personnel scampered to their feet and rushed into the corridor from the door he used. There was a spurt of gunfire down the way, likely from a startled merc. More screams, and the pitter-patter of panicked feet.

Aric had bought some time with a coagulated corridor. He didn't waste a single second.

Eyes scanned, hands gathered.

Like everything else, Aric's heart raced.

4

Never in a million years would a self-respecting Mech pilot regard a payoff in the field as luck. It was good fortune, at best, that a warhead's blast didn't get sucked into their ventilation system, that a PPC impact didn't combust a heatsink, that a well-placed Laser didn't detonate an ammo cache. These things happened all the time, under the aim of experienced and novice pilots alike, *to* experienced and novice pilots alike.

Sometimes an actuator blew despite suffering only 70% damage, and sometimes an actuator withheld at less than 10% integrity and eighty tons of machine bearing down on top of it.

Pure happenstance, half the time.

Some things could be computed, others could not. Such as stumbling across a weapons and munitions disassembly room when Aric was running low on options.

His "luck" didn't end there, though.

Most of the equipment in that room had come from *Mechs*. They weren't defective Imperators and machineguns. They were disassembled Autocannons, innocuous parts to PPCs and Lasers, ammo for LBXs and RACs. The only thing he didn't find in that room were missiles. Not a single SRM, be it a stabilizing fin and certainly not a warhead.

He imagined volatile equipment was tended to in another part of the building.

Under better safety conditions.

Although…he *had* already witnessed several instances of incompetence on the property.

Mathematically speaking, he shouldn't have been able to achieve as much as he did, alone, in a *Shieldmaiden* no less. It wasn't an ideal Mech for a lone-wolf sabotage mission, especially on grounds where more than one enemy Mechs were reported.

Armed with a PPC, RAC, and SRMs, and two medium-bore Lasers, Aric defied all odds in his *Shieldmaiden*. He prioritized structural damage, particularly his marked targets, utilizing his PPC to melt beams and collapse rooftops. His rotary Autocannon suppressed small arms fire from the ground and through windows. His Lasers served virtually no purpose except to engage

Lightweight Mechs, though for the most part he simply eluded the *Cicadas* that eventually tracked him.

Until push came to shove and he neutralized one of them.

Inventoried with twenty-four SRMs, he had put twenty-one to use, detonating ammo caches and fuel dumps two missiles at a time. The last three, unfortunately, never had the privilege of flight. They went down with the *Shieldmaiden*, along with—the number stuck with Aric—55 rounds for his RAC.

Having achieved as much as he did with arguably so little, Aric was ready to prove once more than quality work could be accomplished with low-quantity supplies.

As it turned out, not so much to his surprise anymore, the room he just left behind was in fact sheltering explosive munitions. No warheads, unfortunately, but he might be able to employ his new inventory to a similar effect.

Before exiting the room, Aric performed two tasks in record time. Of course, technically speaking, they were automatic records because he had never done something like this before.

First, he scooped up an empty 20mm casing, sat it on a desk, and ejected three rounds from his SMG. Then he popped the bullets off, using the Cutter's bayonet, and dumped the gunpowder into the casing. He would have added more—wanting at least five—but simply didn't have time. Then he plugged the top with his thumb, slung an eighteen-kilo quilt of LBX ammo over his shoulder, and concisely studied a small map on the wall. For employees in the event of a fire or other emergencies, it served his purpose in as little as five seconds.

When he did dart out of the room, keeping low, he drew the attention of a throng of mechs down the corridor to his right. They had their hands full. Between trying to extinguish the flames in the server room and placating the workers Aric had just dismissed, they weren't in any condition to start shooting.

Not only did he manage to make it down the next corridor without hearing a single shot, but he knew he had a few seconds of extra cushion.

If there was one thing he could count on, it was the remaining *Cicada* pilot.

Two things he had taken under consideration, before following through with this plan.

One—as cruel a thought as it was, most machine-heads who helmed a Lightweight weren't the sharpest tools in the shed. They had a propensity of avoiding common sense and chasing bait with little afterthought.

Of course, the occasional exception existed. Every so often, a talented pilot would accept a temporary job in a Lightweight if it was *given* to them by the employer. Aric had turned down two such jobs in the last three years.

So far, today, under the gray skies of Alzirr, his experience with the *Cicadas* had proven they weren't in this demographic. If nothing else, he could rely on a second condition: the human tendency to fall prey to vengeance. Aric had taken out one of the two *Cicadas*, though part of him hoped the pilot had survived. There was no reason for them not to have. Still, the remaining pilot out there probably had a mind for revenge.

Banking on it, Aric made haste to the nearest exit. His brief study of the map moments ago provided him with a slight advantage. Surely, the mercs pursuing him were not expecting their quarry to deliberately run into the open. Not with a nimble Mech designed for anti-infantry stalking the property.

His only other blessing would be that the *Kodiak* was, in fact, not allowed to actually breach the perimeter. If it was truly hired as an emergency overwatch or outer sentry, he could be sure of this.

The exit door opened with a shove, and for a few seconds Aric was distracted. A rush of wintry air struck him, but given his endurance of heat and sweat this evening, it felt particularly refreshing.

Then the ground beneath him shook minutely, a sensation he knew well enough to be a nearby Mech. The *Cicada* was only a "Lightweight" when compared to its larger kin; the war machine was still a thirty-ton beast that rose twenty feet into the air.

Aric had also counted on the *Cicada* knowing his exact location after blowing the server room. The belch of flame that probably breached the roof had been signal enough.

Aric stood in a tiny alcove in front of the emergency exit, beneath a short awning. He had let the door close behind him, or else he'd be in the mercs' line-of-fire.

This would be his only breather.

He used it.

LBX ammo was stored in "quilts," segmented blankets that looked like a suicide vest. To the uneducated, the 20mm munitions could be misperceived as lead or iron balls, like those used in cannons of old. In reality, they housed clusters of tetranitrate, a compact high-explosive.

One quilt of LBX ammo contained eight rounds. The one he grabbed had six, and would have to do. Thanks to adrenaline, Aric managed carried the eighteen-kilogram quilt like a handkerchief. It was, however, starting to weigh on him.

He peered around the concrete corner of the building, not expecting the *Cicada* to be so close. Less than ten meters. He pulled back, pocketed the casing of gunpowder opening-up, and held the quilt out as if preparing to fold a blanket. Then he took a bottomless breath.

Another stride.

The *Cicada*'s left leg whooshed by, a mere ten feet from his face. The two-toed foot anchored in six inches of snow, and paused. As he moved forward, he heard the Mech's cockpit bow. Unlike most designs, the *Cicada* didn't have a pivotal torso, and would have to adjust its footing to look around.

It was too close to see him.

Aric slung the quilt onto the Mech's left foot, magnetic patches at the top marrying it to the narrow ankle. Used for storing the quilts in ammo depots, Aric now thanked them for a diffcrent purpose.

He then extracted the 20mm casing from his jumpsuit pocket, and began to tilt it—

The *Cicada* took another stride. The left ferrosteel toe almost broke him in half in the process. He felt relief when the quilt stayed in place after the foot set down ten feet away. Aric rushed ahead, reached the foot, and dumped the gunpowder onto the quilt as if a liquid.

Then he backed up, fishing the semiautomatic pistol from his right pocket. The *Cicada*'s other foot lifted to move forward. Aric aimed, fired.

Missed.

"Son of a—"

Aimed, fired.

A brief spark and a nanosecond later, explosions. One collided with the other, and they set off like a volatile bag of popcorn. Armor was lightest at the ankle of any Mech, but on a *Cicada* it was almost like sheet metal. This was usually pardoned because it was virtually impossible to land a crippling blow to such a tiny target on the nimblest Mech ever built.

The quilt of LBX munitions detonated in a flurry of watermelon-sized yellow-orange explosions, and yet Aric thought he could hear the ferrosteel actually crumple in the process. Then metal groaned loudly as the

Cicada completed its stride—planting a footless leg-stump into the snowy mud.

Aric gawked up, backpedaling, as the Mech leaned to the left.

"Well, I'll be," he muttered to himself, allowing a smidgen of pride to get by him.

He was still backpedaling across the snow when the emergency exit door he had used burst open. Two mercs stumbled out into the crisp air, one of them widening his eyes after Aric. His weapon raised, but the other merc grabbed the man's uniform, and redirected his attention.

Then the *Cicada* fell.

Into the maintenance building.

There was a tumultuous crash, and a small wave of flames erupted to swathe the *Cicada* torso. These were put out by the wind alone, and served no grave threat to the pilot inside. Aric only hoped that any non-merc personnel inside the building hadn't been crushed in the process.

He turned on his heels and darted in the opposite direction, before the mercs' shock dissolved.

He reached a generator housing and tried the door, but it was locked. A keypad on the wall beside it emanated a red light. He sidled the tank-sized structure until he found a niche between it and the maintenance building.

Putting his back to it, Aric caught his breath.

The pistol in his hands was fully loaded, save for two rounds. Which meant he had fourteen chances to save his life yet again. To prolong it, though for what reason exactly he wasn't too sure.

How many little victories could he accrue before his enemies got their way?

Aric Vallon wasn't the one-man army he sometimes assured himself he was. The scar that leapt from his left brow to his left cheek was only a vestige of the horrors he witnessed as Fleet infantry when he was nineteen. Twelve years later, and he was on foot again, his least favorite place to be with enemies on his tail. Much less, alone.

That was the path he had chosen, though.

A rogue Mech pilot was seldom trusted, and rarely had the ethos Aric possessed. Or so he had convinced himself.

Whistling and boots in the snow caught his ear. He turned it to the outside, instead of listening to his own subconscious bullshit.

There weren't many options to choose from.

Either continue to navigate the perimeter of this building, or cross an expanse and head toward another. The nearest structure was a thirty-meter dash—in the open. He suspected that if the mercs on his tail had him in their sights, regardless of orders, they would light him up.

And Aric wouldn't blame them.

Still, he had his own calling to obey. The desire to survive. A tenacity he had not forfeit just yet.

5

Athletes get a second wind. Mech pilots, like cats, are theorized to have at least thirteen upon deployment. To deal with the heat waves, sweat, cramped space, vibrations, alarms, and a menagerie of other stressful anxieties that accompany piloting a fifty-plus-ton war machine. Whether Aric was on his third wind or thirteenth, he couldn't be sure. But he was definitely nearing the end of his supply.

The air was thin and coarse.

His lungs weren't faring well out here, as his jumpsuit was about as much cushion to the cold as a raincoat. Beneath it were his skivvies, which counted for nothing in twenty-degree weather.

Deciding against the crossing of an open space between buildings, for the time being Aric chose option B. He would navigate the perimeter of this one until he had a lesser gap to traverse.

Taking advantage of that third or thirteenth wind, Aric gathered his bearings—pistol in his right hand—and left his spot. Snow crunched under his partially melted boot soles. His breaths labored despite stopping to steady his lungs, a faint wheezing sound escaping his lips. He inched toward the next corner, checked left, and then—

Right.

Right into the butt of an Imperator.

The rifle landed, possibly breaking his nose. He staggered back, pain and heat enveloping his face. Not the kind of warmth he wanted to be blanketed in. Dizzied, his gaze danced around before dropping. He spotted the steel-toed boots of a mercenary, and then the dapple of crimson on snow.

Under the whistle of a cutting breeze, Aric heard a trigger depress. Halfway. Someone stopped it, and then two men exchanged words in private. One of them was especially angry.

Aric smiled; part of his brain worried it would be his last one on this plane.

The rest of his brain was satisfied with that.

"Orders are orders," the gruff voice said.

Aric continued to watch his nose drip blood and mucous onto the snow. Two feet from the gun he had dropped.

And then another blow caught his forehead, and he didn't have a chance to feel pain before darkness swallowed him.

***

The last time he was cradled by the void, it was relatively short-lived and, technically, self-inflicted. This time, he had a particular, albeit nameless, merc to thank. And time passed, apparently, swifter than he expected.

When he came to, it was at the aid of several men shaking him violently.

A series of jagged coughs rattled out of his lungs and mouth, before the black rucksack covering his head was pulled off.

Jarring light barraged him from above. Other than that LED umbrella, the room was dark. Claustrophobic to any man except him. A Mech pilot would laugh at the interrogation tactic. As he wanted to, but the searing pain in his skull stopped him.

Steel-toed boots tapped the aluminum legs of the chair he was bound to, as the merc circled behind him. A fistful of his short hair was seized, then his head yanked back, and a blade drawn. It made a distinct sound when shocked from its sheath. As Aric's vision corrected, his glimpsed a glimmer against the polished metal, skipping off the serrations.

A wry smirk adorned his face, painfully.

He tasted blood on his gums.

Only a merc of such poor taste would wield a polished Bowie, and not a carbon steel dirk. Aric pitied the man.

Even as he felt the tickle of his weapon's serrations on his throat.

Three men loomed into view before him, Aric having to stare down his cheeks to see their silhouettes. The one in the middle stepped closer to him than the others. His breath reeked—

Or was that Aric's own sweat?

This damn jumpsuit.

It had been through hell, and now Aric was facing its gatekeepers.

"You've been a horrible thorn in my side all evening, you know?"

An accent he couldn't place. Trionian?

On the plus side, the closer the man leaned forward, the less the harsh the light above him seemed.

Aric tried to speak, but the presence of the merc's blade just above his Adam's apple made it tough. Apparently the leader of his captors noticed, and with two fingers signaled the merc to ease up. The knife was withdrawn, but his head remained pulled back.

"Say, who hired you? Was it, uh, the Fleet? They've never really...condoned my businesses. Not here, not in Trion."

Aric's smirk flickered.

"Your machine, such a waste. Tsk-tsk." The barren humor in the man's voice became an irritant to Aric's ears. "Care to elaborate, perhaps? A saving grace, before I let my men decide your fate?"

Aric tried not to scoff.

His mouth hurt.

"I see. Then you shall die nameless. Is that what you want? No legacy? The man, solely responsible for *fucking up my operation*!?"

A sudden outburst, Aric wasn't expecting after so much wit and composure. Now Aric really did grin. A laugh vibrated his throat and he swallowed the pain, along with what tasted like a quarter pint of blood.

A rancid, coppery gasp exited his mouth and repelled the man.

He gestured at the merc behind Aric, and his hair was released. Aric's head bobbed between his shoulders before he mustered the strength to raise it. Only slightly at first, as blood dribbled from his lower gums, over a split lip and onto his lap.

"Men like you…wouldn't know what to do with a *legacy*. Your ears, they don't deserve…to know my name."

"Sir, let me pull his filthy tongue out of his throat and be done with him. He's wasted enough of our time to begin with."

The merc behind him, Aric's only regret now was that he had not given him a quick death. Quicker, anyway, than whatever life was going to deal him. A shame than men of such low merit breathed the same air of those far worthier.

"No, even that would be a waste of energy," the leader said. He stepped aside and whistled curtly at someone behind him, then snapped his fingers.

Another man stepped forward, but paused.

The leader spoke again.

"Pathetic. Mercenaries." He scoffed. "Pilots for hire are a dime-a-dozen. You won't be missed; less money your employer has to pay."

Then he stepped aside and the other man advanced, but he stopped midstride when Aric began laughing. It came from the gut at first, rising from a baritone to a wheezing snicker. Slowly, he lifted his head to squint under the harsh white light and sneer at those surrounding him.

Despite his disturbingly raucous laugh, he now spoke in an even tone that should have conveyed even more concern.

"The simplicity of having a goal and achieving it, on the precipice of assured death, why, it's the most satisfying way to live one's life." Then he scoffed himself, smirking through it. "Of course, you would know nothing of this. You work not for honor, but money."

Aric Vallon spit at the man's tattered boots, a wad of saliva and blood slinking to the floor.

"*You* are mercs first, before anything," he said. "I am a *warrior* first."

The men were stunned, but the one closest to him was not past action. He wielded a pistol, and racked the slide. Aric didn't register the gunshot, nor did his blood-framed grin waver the slightest.

www.ingramcontent.com/pod-product-compliance
Lightning Source LLC
Chambersburg PA
CBHW071520110726
47908CB00003B/903